Conspiracy
of
Doves

Conspiracy of Doves

by Helen Conner

To Cristina

Thank you for being
a dove among hawks

love
Helen

To order additional copies of this book, contact:
Xlibris
800-056-3182
www.Xlibrispublishing.co.uk
Orders@Xlibrispublishing.co.uk
756080

Cat caught a glimpse of the new moon between two high buildings. It was tipped, slanted, like a saucer having milk spilled from it.

She weighed her fatigue, the size of the bundle she carried, the distance she had let grow between herself and her mother's heels - and then she realised this could be her last chance for a long time, stopped weighing things and ran, stumbling a little, to catch up with her mother.

When she got there, she had no breath to speak, just glanced sideways at the new moon, let her eyes implore - a little, not too much.

Her mother followed her eyes, then smiled her rare smile, a little crooked, a little wry.

"Crescent moon up in the sky,
"She follow we home, you and I -
"But she don't be walking, she lie back at ease,
"She don't got to hurry, she do as she please,
"Only look down on us just for to tease,
"As we hurry home, you and I."

Cat frowned. Her mother's voice was full of heavy sadness, so that she was almost sorry she'd pulled her away from whatever she'd been thinking about, marching on ahead like she had.

She let herself fall behind again, wondering what was going through her mother's mind.

The clothes they carried were from the bawdy house. She knew her mother hated doing business with them - hated more when the only way they could find money enough for rent, for food, for protection, was to go into one of the upstairs rooms.

Today there had been one man, rich, soft, and the madam had stayed the whole time. He hadn't touched either of them - hadn't tested the copper curl of Cat's hair against the black twist of her mother's, hadn't tweaked the corner of her dress to see if the skin beneath was white, not amber, or licked a finger and rubbed at her mother's skin, to see what might come off.

He had just looked, said, "Yes - yes, I do see what you mean," and waved a hand in dismissal.

Cat had always hated going into the upstairs rooms - it made her feel like a dog set to fight a bear, over-matched and knowing it. Afterwards, she had trouble looking at her mother, and knew it would be a long time before she'd get her mother to look straight at her.

But it was money - and money was always good. And she could ask her mother for anything afterwards, because they would be the Only Two. If she asked her mother to carry her home, she would pick her up, her and both bundles, and stagger down the street a few steps before spilling her burdens, daughter and laughter and all, into the muddy street.

But she was chin-high to her mother now - she'd decided not to play that game again until she was strong enough to carry her mother and both bundles, and be the one to stagger and laugh.

"You got somewhere else to go?"

She'd walked straight by her mother - straight past the alley that led to their door. She ducked past her mother, lifted the string that opened the door, and made her way straight to bed. She disposed the bundle carefully, pillow and bolster both, and watched her mother through slitted eyes as she sorted through her bundle - this to soak, this to scrub, this to handle later when they'd feel as fragile as the flimsy things that would tolerate no soaking, no scrubbing.

When her mother had finished the first bundle, she'd have to take over. Unless she wanted to play the 'only two' card early. If she held onto it, it might be worth more. If she held onto it, it might be trumped by some real or imagined reason for her mother to turn against her.

She let herself believe she'd play the card until her mother had finished altogether with her bundle - and then she rolled off the bed, hauled her bundle over, and started the long job of sorting.

"Tell me about my father," she said. Best time to ask this question was when she was firmly African - give it a few days, she'd be the half-white ingrate again, you wait, you'll see.

"Your father? He was a big man. Big in all ways. And - a king among men. Generous. Warm. But warm as England sun - not warm like sun of Afric. He gave me gold to live on for years after he sent me from him..."

Cat kept her attention carefully on her work. To ask questions was to invite rebuke. Rebuke followed by long silence.

Her silence was rewarded. "If I was still with him - ah, you'd have mothers courting you for their fine sons. Boys dressed like peacocks, with emeralds on their pinkie the colour of your eyes..."

Cat made herself breathe evenly, and act like nothing in the world was more important than this sad thing in her hands that some woman would be wearing in two days time - hardly enough to keep out the cold...

The women went into the bawdy houses fine and strong, and they came out broken. So much money flowed towards them, and it seemed like they were chained on a rock, with nothing to do but be beaten at and steadily chilled by waves of wealth, all the time waiting for a dragon to show up.

She hated her life, often enough, nothing but work and worry. Still, year on year, she and her mother got stronger and cleverer, better at charming the wolf away from their door, towards someone else's.

Her mother was talking again - she put her chain of thought up onto a shelf in her mind, to be taken down and knit at later.

"Your eyes... green as a leaf in spring, they are. Who needs emeralds with eyes like that?"

Cat was perturbed. What had happened to the fine boys with their ambitious mothers? What had happened to the palaces and fine riding horses her mother would usually have reached by now, if she hadn't sunk already into a dejected silence?

Nice as it was to have pretty eyes - it hardly outweighed all of that.

Cat swung down the road, her bundle perched neatly on her hip. She looked back over her shoulder, and realised she was losing her mother again. It was odd - the old king had died, the young king on his throne looked fair to be the granting of universal wishes. Everyone rejoiced - but her mother alone had become - not old. She was not even near old - but she had begun to seem a particular age, not young, where once she had seemed eternal, unchanging.

Her boundless energy, her limitless determination seemed to falter, now and then.

Cat smiled a little to herself, slowing her steps until her mother was beside her again.

"You want be carried?" she asked slyly.

She stayed a decent distance away from her mother while her mother walked the wavering line between anger and laughter, between indignation and gratitude.

Finally, her mother laughed, and she laughed with her.

"Tchah!" was all her mother said, but it was good. Mad over happy - not happy over mad.

"So. Fourth chick - tell me about her."

This was a new game between them.

Old times, her mother would tell her of Eagle and her three chicks, how Eagle had to fly away from a storm, and could only take one chick to safety. How she asked each chick in turn what they would do for her when they were grown. How the first one offered first pick of her meals when she was grown, and was dropped to her death on the rocks below.

How second chick offered to save her mother from the storm when she was grown - and was dropped to her own death.

How third chick promised to do the same for her own chick if she ever had to - and was carried away to safety.

Cat would listen and try to ask questions that would be heard right, and steer clear of questions that would be heard wrong.

Recently, she'd decided to ask a question she'd been steering clear of back almost as far as she could remember.

"If there had been a fourth chick - would Eagle have saved third chick? Did she get the right answer, or did Eagle just save her so she'd have at least something to work with while she was breeding three new chicks?"

Her mother had stayed quiet a scary long time, and then said "Hah!" scary loud. "I never once thought of that! All those years I heard that story told, I just assumed last answer was right answer. What answer would fourth chick give?".

And she had sounded genuinely curious, like she wanted to hear an answer, not like she was waiting to pounce on an answer and dismember it.

Since then, they'd found out a lot about fourth chick. She was limitless in her ambitions, while neat in her nest. She was polite to the elderly, but would stand her ground against injustice. She would one day make a fine grandmother.

Cat bit her lip, not anxious, just searching to find exactly the right chunk of her world to hand over to her mother, her other, her otherme. When she was mother, near ready to be grandmother, what would she want to hear?

And what would offend her, coming from a mere chit of a girl, young enough to be her own daughter?

The truth was, she was an age to start having daughters now, and wondering more and more how her mother came to have one child, and no father to point to. Was she raped? Was that why she was sometimes angry with Cat, for no reason Cat could figure out? Was she deceived? Had she fled a man who beat her, or wanted to sell her?

So many questions, and she knew fourth chick was about to start spilling them all over. She'd about run out of tactful ways to end the story.

She looked straight at her mother.

"You know, most chicks my age, have chicks of their own now. Or, at least, a big male eagle somewhere near the nest..."

"Oh."

"I'm not - it's not -"

She stopped, knowing her mother was unforgiving of less than perfect English. At least when they were out where others could hear them. At home - at home she might even fall into the sweet cadences of her own mothertongue - which Cat could understand not even a jot of, but loved, as she loved all music.

"Had you met my father when you were my age?" she asked, finally, not making any pretence of being fourth chick.

"When I was your age, I was still in Italy. From Italy to France - that took almost another year. From France to England - I met your father when I was about two winters older than you are now. He was - he was tall, and beautiful for a man. Well read - courteous. I couldn't see then that..."

"That...?"

"Child, no man is perfect in every way. He had a weakness. Hard to see when you first looked - all you saw was tall, and strong, and charming. But he had a weakness, still and all."

There was a finality in her voice, more than in her words. And, they were home.

Cat held the door open so her mother could duck under, then was caught behind her mother when she didn't immediately walk in. Just a second - but long enough for her to realise there was something amiss - like the time when their small store of gold had been gone, and her mother had known it before even looking in the hiding place.

That had been a bad day - her mother had accused her, then consoled her, then accused her, then consoled her. Eventually, she'd worked out that if Cat had taken the gold, Cat would have a new dress, a new doll, or enough candy plums to make her vomit for a week.

Even then - they'd both known that would be a hard winter, no store of wealth to let them idle a week if the roads were ice and mire, or buy a new song, or pay off any new men who chanced along, and thought they looked like there was profit in them.

Cat sidled round her mother, felt her heart sink down inside her like a stone through a pond. There was a man sitting in the one seat, the one where you could warm yourself by the fire (once it was lit) and catch the best of the sun through the gap in the wall above (always supposing it rose high enough to reach in at all).

Flanking him, two men who were irrelevant, really. They wouldn't act without orders from him - and Cat already knew that to be true of herself as long as he was in the room. It shamed her, it troubled her - she wanted to be obedient to no man.

She'd seen him only once before. He'd never laid hands on her, but his eyes had bruised her enough.

She waited for her mother to attack or retreat or negotiate. After a time, she chanced a sideward glance at her mother's face.

She had thought she could not feel more shamed - but her mother's docile patience in the face of this situation shamed her more than her own. This was the person who had cowed her for years, sometimes with sweet words, sometimes with shouting? This quiet nothing-person?

She put her gaze down to the floor, and made herself remember that there was more than sweet words and shouting between them. There was laughter, and hard lessons, and shared warmth on the coldest winter nights. She would have to watch herself - keep some part of her free of the spell this man cast with his eyes. Her body would have to obey him - her mind should obey her.

"Take the older one to the house in Southwark. She should do well there."

Cat made herself speak. "Sir - where my mother goes, I go too."

The sudden blow shocked her. She had looked for violence from him, from his cronies - but her mother had never hit her openly in front of strangers - not once, though she had walked home with her many times knowing violence waited for her.

"You'd walk of your own will into a bawdy house? What are you - born stupid or born whore?"

Cat drew a sharp breath in. Her mother turned to the man, bowed her head meekly.

"I am sorry for the girl's impudence. Lord knows I've tried to knock it out of her, these many years. She got an older body than she got a head, if you wise to see that. She will go with you, and do your will." And she cast a look sideways at Cat that said 'don't shame me'.

Cat wanted to laugh. What could she possibly do that would shame her mother more than her mother had shamed herself? Shamed Cat along with her?

"If you please, sir - we have been long working, and if we have a journey ahead of us, you should let us tend ourselves. The yard has tall walls - and you can send a man after us, if you fear we can fly."

"I've seen your walls - I'd worry more about you burrowing through the midden under them. When I grow bored, I'll send a man after you - you have until then."

Cat followed her mother, feeling her mouth set sullen, her eyes going flat.

"So, what are we here for, mother?" she asked once the door was between them and the man.

"What I said - I have never lied to that man, and never will. A fool lies in front of the lord of lies, and I was never that."

Cat shook her head, but the habit of obedience took her to the midden which took all the refuse of their house, and gave back dock and fireweed and faerie trumpet.

"I will tell you this, and tell you it once. If you walk of your own will into the house where I go now, you are no daughter of mine from that day on."

"But you will walk in there ready enough - what does that make you? Born stupid, or born whore?"

Cat held her breath, waiting for the next blow to fall on her, was shocked by her mother's sudden laughter.

"It makes me that man's property," she said.

"Is he my father?" she asked, small-voiced. She'd been wondering that, off and on, for years, for he was many of the things her mother described in her father - and who did not change over the course of their life, losing sweetness, gaining bitter?

Her mother laughed again.

"No. He is the man who sold me to your father. Had you been a son, your father's will would have left both of us to each other. As you are a daughter, he left both of us back to him. We have been his for some weeks now."

Cat grew wide-eyed - then caught herself. "You must have prayed for a son," she said, formal and quiet.

"Fool girl - what I prayed for, I got in front of me. You finished?"

"Long since," said Cat, confused.

"Then I count my whole life a worthwhile thing, and we better go. That man get bored faster than most, and Southwark not so far from here."

Cat scrambled to put her clothing to rights, and followed her mother back into the house. So much, so much she wanted to ask, questions stumbling over each other, as she stumbled over her feet, rushing into the house so fast, she arrived with her dress still above her knees, to general laughter.

Her mother could put a weapon inside a honeyed word - none better. But that voice she used - that was her end of day voice. Day done, and part done well, part done badly - but now come rest. Cat found herself in tears, turned about by her mother, wrapping her brisk in a shawl, pushing her into the hands of one of the tall men, so fast it was hard to notice that under the shawl were two things: the copy her mother had of the new king's bible, and the doll her mother made her, many years ago, cloth from her mother's dress to wrap it, hair from her mother's head to cover its head.

She hardly noticed the moment when she saw her mother last - had she been bundled out first, and into the waiting carriage? Had her mother walked out, erect, accompanied by one of the men? She was so preoccupied with the riddle her mother had handed her - and perhaps that was, in the end, the point of it.

Cat leaned her cheek against the glass of the window, listening for the raucous laughter of the fowl on the distant lake.

She rested one soft hand on her book, the other held her doll against her. She wasn't looking at either - drifting, bored, letting her mind travel out and out, as her body never could. She saw others walk round the lake - she was not permitted past the door of this room.

For company, twice a day, she had the girls who brought her food and fresh clothing, took away dirty dishes and her covered pot. If she greeted either girl in any way, or had not tied the mask provided onto her face before they arrived, those girls would disappear, to be replaced by others.

It had been a long time since she tested that hypothesis - now, she just listened to their chatter, hoping for clues, understanding that any clues provided could as easy be lie as truth.

Still, there were, twice a day, two voices to hear, two faces to watch sidelong through the soft muslin of her eye mask. Over the rest of her face was thicker cloth, so that, to them, she must look a strange creature indeed, stranger than the doll she held, which had, at least, recognisable features, a mouth, eyes, hair.

The book and doll had been taken from her once - held for about a sennight, then returned. She read the book openly, and one of the times she had risked speech, she had wondered aloud if she might be allowed writing materials. The writing materials had not been granted - both girls had gone, replaced by others.

She imagined herself outside the glass, looking in. The glass was thick and cobbled, of course, set in neat diamonds separated by lead, but she could imagine it clear as air, showing her a princess, hair neatly brushed, sitting on a silken cushion looking out at beautiful gardens.

She sighed. Better to be a washer-girl. Better by far. If she'd known that wealth would mean, to her, this closeted existence, one book to read (and how she regretted those times she had turned down her mother's offer to teach her from it! How she longed for anyone's opinion of it that might differ, in any respect, from her own), one doll to speak to, and that in hushed tones lest her words endanger those approaching her door...

She wandered her memory hoping for any hint of a tale where Cinders found her way out of the castle, back to her old life, full of struggle and spite as it had been... happy ever after was a bore.

There came a tap on the door: interesting. It wasn't time for the girls to enter, chattering - that was always morning.

She didn't call out - she wasn't in particularly a spiteful day this day. Be something interesting she willed at the shut door. Be something that will carry me through three or four days of speculation and pondering.

It was the girls. They changed her clothes - this perfectly pleasant dress which would look not out of place in any of the places Cat had ever been, for some odd thing of strange materials, which left strange places bare to the air, while covering up others much more accustomed to seeing daylight. Cat's mask, linen and muslin, they left perfectly undisturbed.

Well: this would make material for a good month of pondering, decently paced. She stepped forwards as they tugged on her hand - bells jingled at her ankles, her wrists, her bosom... She smiled beneath the veil, resting one hand on her navel, her bosom and legs being... well, feeling decently covered, even though she could tell each ray of sunlight shone straight through the flimsy material that covered them.

Elizabeth was weary already, sick to death of smiling and smiling and smiling. And this... thing at the foot of the steps, face swathed in black linen, body hardly decently covered. And the skin - all that skin, the colour of her old pony - surely that had to be paint of some kind?

Her ex-lover: ex-step-father: ex-friend: ex-honourable enemy... would-be controller smiled at her from one step behind the odd object, reached to begin removing the mask that obscured its features.

For no truly understood reason, she did not want to look at its face. Could think of no expressable reason why she should order it removed, mask intact.

"We - do not accept your gift. It looks very like a person - a young person, at that. Have it returned to its mother."

"It is not so young. It has been absent from its mother since your brother died."

The unwinding continued inexorably. She knew she could not show weakness - not while that man was in the room. He still harboured hopes of being her husband, de-facto King of England. There had been a time when she could conceive of no higher bliss than to be alone in a room with this man. Now the thought made vomit rise into her throat.

It was like a very bad dream. The linen was lifted back, leaving muslin behind it: he reached to lift the muslin and she saw - a moment before the others in the room, she saw the threat.

"How amusing. Like receiving an ancient cameo that, by chance, captures the look of a family member."

She had spoken just soon enough that her words reached the people in the room before the muslin was drawn back - before they saw that this person was, indeed, a copy of her own self. Less costly, perhaps - drawn in amber upon amber, jade-eyed, not ruby and pearl, sapphire-eyed.

"With the mask removed, it looks younger still. Please do remove it - as I said, we are not accustomed to own persons."

"Highness, this is no more a person than the capuchin monkey that rests on that man's shoulder: the parrot adorning that woman's wrist. It has a voice of sorts - but no true intelligence."

"Highness..."

He was right - its voice sounded broken, harsh, as if being used for the first time. Very like the voice of that parrot he had pointed out. And, the only word it had spoken mimicked the first word he spoke.

"Highness - my mother would wish me to serve you."

"Is that so? She told you as much?"

"She told me to obey this man: and then to obey the person into whose hands he put me. He puts me into your hands - my mother's will is that I be of service to you."

"Show me your hands."

It held out two brown paws, showing old callus, short nails... odd. The nails themselves had that strange, hennaed tint.

"Highness, there is a story my mother told me - let me tell it to you."

"Speak." Doubtless it was well-rehearsed by its current owner - yet he didn't have that look of overweening satisfaction she had learned to look for as one of his plans unfolded.

It spoke. Best pay attention.

"Once was a mother eagle, had three chicks. Came a storm, and mother eagle took first chick, largest, best chick out over the water, flying to safety. Mother eagle ask: I do this for you, child - what you do for me when storm come next? Chick answer: I carry you from storm, like you carry me. First chick drop to its death on the rocks below.

Elizabeth let her impatience show - a small matter of breath and a movement of shoulders - and to its credit, it caught the signal and spoke faster, visibly omitted repetition.

"Second chick answer: I will give you first pick of my kills. Second chick die. Third chick answer: I will carry my own chick far from the storm, as you carry me. Third chick live."

"And?"

"And - there is more to this story which I will tell - when the only others in the room are those you would trust with your life, those who guard your sleep and your food."

"I will tell you tonight - and if you are disappointed, I'll leave, no quarrel."

Elizabeth weighed her options. She could keep the girl close, and watch her for signs of curiosity or deceit.

"Agreed," she said, lifting her chin a little. She had decided before now that there were times when she could not know if she would be right or wrong. The trick then was to decide: which was the right way to be wrong? In this case, if she was wrong to let the girl stay, at least the lesson would be a conclusive one. If the girl left, there would be no lesson, so she gestured the girl to sit, the first of many tests, and noted that she hesitated only a little before settling herself, with reasonable grace, on the ground near Elizabeth, facing out.

The day was long. Elizabeth was impressed by the girl's patience and stamina. At last the time came to retire to her rooms, where Kempe and Newbury waited. She paused to allow the girl to follow her, but did not speak. She had played fair to all who came - now she had no more strength for putting at ease and making welcome.

In her room, she chose a chair, and sat carefully, not letting her exhaustion show.

"So - there was more to this story of yours."

"True - and for you and those you trust to hear. If there is one you would trust with a knife to your throat, I would say they should hear it - else it is for you alone."

Elizabeth did not allow herself to pause noticeably. The right way to be wrong was with total conviction.

"Both of these women can be trusted absolutely."

"That is good. So - once there was a Queen Eagle, who had four chicks."

"Four? You said three."

"True, Highness. Somerset will never know about fourth chick. If I wanted to tell him, I couldn't - the words would bounce off him. So I thought best not to rub his nose in what he can't ever have."

Elizabeth laughed - short and weary, but more real than any other that day.

"Highness?"

"How would you rub someone's nose in something they can't have?"

"True, Highness. You have a good mind."

Elizabeth sighed. More flattery - who would have thought that sweet words would cloy so after a day of hearing little else?

"And can I say, I've now fulfilled one of my purposes."

Elizabeth caught her breath a little - perhaps now she would see the girl's true colours.

"Wasn't that the first real laugh you've had today? And there will be more, I promise."

"Continue with the story. Start from where the Queen takes the fourth chick across the ravine."

"Highness," the girl chided, "A story is defined by its ending - but without the beginning the end has no meaning. You say you trust these women with your life, yet you would cheat them of something that would cost you only time? What does that tell us about you, Highness? More important - what does that tell you about you?"

Elizabeth added that into the debt column, which was growing longer, and only a brief laugh to balance it.

"As you will, but be as brief as may be - I feel a headache beginning."

"Highness. May I rub your shoulders and neck? I used to do that for my mother - she'd like me to do it for you."

Elizabeth beckoned, sat straighter still, and closed her eyes as the girl's strong, cool fingers found knots of poison and eased them away. She let the first part of the story wash over her, not really attending, until Kempe said, "Rather a hapless mother, don't you think?"

The girl's hands stilled. Elizabeth opened her eyes, and began to listen again to the girl's voice.

"Pray, when you say that, that you never have to make hard decisions about your own children. And while you do, pray for the women who must make those decisions. We'd all be born in a castle if we could be."

Elizabeth swivelled. "How long since you saw your mother, child?"

"Many months now."

"I saw my mother perhaps four times that I remember. It is not all pleasure to live in a castle - in some ways, you are a deal luckier than I, and I would have you remember it."

The girl opened her mouth as if to answer, then lowered her eyes, and inclined her head. Elizabeth turned. "Continue," she said.

"So. Queen Eagle flies back to the nest to take up fourth chick. 'Chick,' says she 'if I do this for you - what will you do for me?' 'Mother,' says fourth chick, 'I will grow strong as I can, and fast as I may, and if the storm come for me, as it came for you, I will be strong enough and fast enough to save all my chicks.' And Queen Eagle fly, strong, and fast, and content with her small chick, high and far from the storm."

The girl came round to kneel before Elizabeth.

"Highness - you have more chicks than Queen Eagle dreamed of, and I know your wish for them - that they be free, that they fly. I am a good person - I am here, truly to help you. With my help, you can save more of your chicks than you could on your own. I have studied, and I know many things - I know Abimelech's secret, and the truth about Lot's daughters, and his sons. And first let me say this - Somerset is not a good man. He will never show you his true face, because you have power and can show him favour. I am nothing to him - so I have seen all of his true face, and he means you no more good than he does me."

"Thank you for that - however, I knew it already. I was not always the most powerful person in whatever game Somerset was playing.

"You may stay for a time - at least until I have considered what is best to do with you. Leave now - Kempe will find you a place to sleep."

Elizabeth gazed out over the audience chamber. She glanced briefly down at the girl who knelt beside her and frowned. She liked to make decisions boldly, and liked even better for it to be seen that she made decisions boldly. Yet from day to day she changed her mind about keeping this girl here, or sending her to a convent, or back to Somerset, for despite all her protests and pretty fables, she could not be certain the girl was not his creature, still.

There was the matter of her upbringing. The briefest questioning had raised the point of her mother's whereabouts - in a bawdy house! And worse, the girl had thought Elizabeth might be persuaded to bring her mother here from that place. She showed, it is true, the sentiment of loyalty towards her mother - yet if her loyalty held to such poor beginnings, what true judgement could she show?

She had, it was true, sought word of the girl's mother for her own satisfaction - but to no avail. It seemed that it had become fashionable to have one piece of exotica in each house, and to watch all of them in the hope of shedding light on one - not to be contemplated.

She had taken well to the plainer, more dignified dress that Elizabeth had insisted upon. However, despite great persuading - and a few beatings - she insisted on washing those clothes herself, which could not but take her into unsavoury company.

She said that it was partly for Elizabeth's own good that she spent time in the company of her least servants - not to spy on them, for that would be odious (Elizabeth had quietly smiled at this ingenuous declaration) but rather to know their minds and concerns, that Elizabeth might not offend them unknowing.

"They are exceptionally well rewarded for workers of their kind, I don't think I should worry over-much about offending them."

"Highness, do you mean well-rewarded with money?"

Elizabeth had frowned - the girl would not learn to have the least delicacy of manner.

"If that is how you must put it."

"Highness, you cannot buy loyalty. Loyalty can only be earned, and to know someone's concerns is to earn much of their loyalty."

"Yet, you will agree, I cannot ask these women to work for me for loyalty's sake. Coin is what they require, not profusions of sentiment. Show me a washerwoman who refuses coin, and offers to serve me for love alone, and I believe I could show you a spy who expects a great reward from my enemy for delivering my life to him."

"Highness, I do not suggest you should withhold coin from any who honestly serve you. But the coin buys their service alone - their honesty must be earned by your own, and not otherwise."

Elizabeth had wearied of the discussion at that point. She had turned to Kempe to beat the girl into obedience - a task Kempe had relished perhaps over-much - and the girl had borne the beating patiently without going on to avow greater obedience in future.

"Highness, I must do what I must do. If I cannot be true to myself, how can I be true to you?"

She had skilled hands. Many a time she had rubbed away the beginnings of a megrin. Yet Elizabeth felt it betokened a weakness in herself if she kept the girl here for only that reason. It was like the sweetmeats that were now so readily available to her. They became noisome, and yet her hand would wander to the bowl almost of itself, if the bowl be near.

She smiled a little. The girl wore the aspect of frankness, and wore it well, whatever was concealed beneath. While others pressed sweetmeats upon her, with pretty phrases to sweeten them the more, the girl had waited until none other was present, and chided her for succumbing so often.

What had she called them? Yes, a snare.

"Not a true pleasure, Highness. You remember, we sang the other night? You taught us that song, 'Rose', and we sang it round a dozen ways, and then you said, 'Enough of singing', and the singing stopped. And if we'd kept on, that would be too much, yes? Tell true, Highness - with these things," and she gestured contemptuously at the bowl, "with these things, enough is still coming after too much is already here. Not so? That is how you tell the snare from the true pleasure. You've had too much, but enough is not yet here."

Since then, she had succumbed less often, and felt the better for it.

There was that to be said for her - she said what none other would say, either because they feared to displease her, or because they had all been tutored the same way, and this untutored girl saw things from another side.

In her favour, also, she kept her silence in court, speaking out only when she was alone with Elizabeth.

If she were to keep her, the girl would need a name. She favoured 'Philomena'. Yet she would not name her until she was certain to keep her here.

A thing that went both ways was her taste for the fantastic. It was diverting to watch her have Kempe hold an orange aloft - and this should be kept still - then have Newbury spin an apple, and while spinning it, progress stately around the orange that Kempe held, and then she must tip the apple, and still it should spin: Elizabeth had found that amusing, even before Newbury fell laughing, in a tangle of skirts and fruit. But the girl had stretched the thing too far.

"And that is why England sun is now hot and now cold, while Afric sun is always warm. My mother learned this thing when she was in Italy, and she told it to me."

Elizabeth's amusement had died there. She supposed that the girl truly believed that her mother had been to Italy, and Spain, and Africa and France - but it saddened her that she had so little knowledge of the reality of the world that she had swallowed her mother's stories whole, and now mixed them with things she heard daily in court.

She sighed, and rested her chin upon her hand. The girl, meanwhile, sat stoic as a hound beside the throne. If only she were truly as trustworthy as a hound.

She sighed again, and gestured for the approach of the young man who waited to speak to her.

Truthfully, he was no younger than she, yet she was so hemmed round by gray beards, that his smooth cheeks were startling to her eye. She was careful to keep her gaze dispassionate, while inwardly she savoured the blue of his eye, the black of his hair. She decided there and then, that whatever his petition, it would be granted, so long as he would stay and lend his council to her. Perhaps she did not need the girl to see things differently - perhaps it was simply youth she wanted near her.

"Highness, I am Dudley of Essex. I have come with a simple request - but first," He hesitated, until she gestured that he should continue. "I pray I will not give offence - but I could not help but notice the beauty of the girl who sits beside you?"

Elizabeth smiled. She approved his tone, and the subtlety of a compliment directed to one who shared her face but not her elevated position. She inclined her head gently and was amused to see him sigh with relief, unguarded as a boy. Unguarded as her brother had often been, alone with Elizabeth.

"I am come to the court at the request of my mother. She would have me be of service to you."

The almost clumsy speed with which he bowed saved Elizabeth from showing him the light in her eyes.

"Girl? Come and rub my shoulders. Girl?"

Elizabeth had sent the girl away to rest. She had less need of her council now, and had begun to rue the attention she had paid to such chancy wisdom. But she could hardly ask Essex to rub her shoulders, and until she felt ready to send the girl to a convent, it could do no harm to avail herself of her gifts on occasion.

The girl had used to come when she called - her room was not far away. She thought about sending Kempe to fetch her, but then thought again. She'd not seen the inside of the girl's room - perhaps it would speed her decision to look on it. She gestured Kempe to hold her place when she would have followed - she could do this alone, there was little enough that could be said of these days.

"Girl?" She eased open the door, feeling oddly apprehensive. Yet the palace was hers, as all England was hers - no door in it could be barred to her.

The girl sat with her back to Elizabeth, intent over something. Elizabeth cast a glance quickly round the room - it was small, the mat the girl sat on almost filled it, and beside her - Elizabeth shuddered - a mannikin of some kind, with a formless face, and a dark, wiry substance serving as hair.

"Girl?" Her voice betrayed her, emerging as a hoarse whisper. This was absurd, to feel this way in her own halls. She took a deep breath, drew in her skirts, and advanced into the room, sidling a little not to brush the wall.

The girl held a roughly made book in her hands, and was peering intently at it.

"What is that?" Elizabeth asked, kindly enough.

"Highness! I did not hear you. It is your brother's bible - see?"

Elizabeth felt chilled with shock. "My brother's what?"

"His bible."

"Who gave it to you? Where did you come by it? It is mine by right - give it to me!"

The girl held the book out, frowning slightly, clearly not seeing the enormity of what she had done. When she held it in her hands, she turned a few pages, seeing childish writing on some of the pages - it was an old thing this, years before he took the throne, her brother's handwriting had improved vastly from this. Yet if it had ever known his touch, it was precious to her thereby, and she felt soiled that the girl's rough paws had handled it.

"You should not have had this."

"Highness?"

The look of dumb incomprehension on the girl's face was more than she could bear.

"Tell me," she strove to be calm, "Tell me that you are sorry you took this. Tell me that, please."

"Highness - I cannot do that."

"Why will you not do that?"

"Highness, I swore when I came here that I would speak only truth to you. I am not sorry to have had your brother's bible - why would I be? It has kept me company. I have been often glad of it."

Elizabeth knew better than to shout and storm with rage - that was her father's way, and she had always hated it. She grew still, and icy.

"Tell me something, then. Tell me something it would grieve you to have someone take from you."

The girl did not speak, but her eyes spoke, resting briefly on the mannikin beside her before she shook her head and began again to speak.

Elizabeth ignored her words, held out her hand, sure her meaning was clear. The girl stopped speaking, sat still and silent. Elizabeth felt her rage grow greater still, and fought for control.

She stooped - feeling every second how wrong it was to stoop before this creature, adding every second of injured pride to the tally of her wrongdoing - and took the mannikin.

"When you will tell me - when you have brought yourself to understand - how wrong you were to take this book, then I will return this thing to you. Not before. Do you understand?"

She knew a moment's remorse at the girl's look of dumb incomprehension, but would not turn aside from what she knew to be right. The girl must learn that the property of others, even - especially - the property of the dead, was not to be lightly taken. She must know in her own heart what it was to lose something she treasured, before there was any hope of her understanding the wrong she had done.

She left the room, knowing that megrin was now inevitable, and no remedy for it. Which meant the decision was made - the girl would go to a convent. But first she must see and confess her wrongdoing - she would send no jackdaw among gentle women.

It was days later when the girl asked to be admitted to her room. During that time, Elizabeth had made clear to the guards that the girl was to be given plain food and water only, and anything necessary was to be taken in to her, and taken away. Elizabeth had not seen her, but had yielded to Essex's petition that he should visit her.

The esteem she held him in grew ever greater - nor Kempe nor Newbury, who had laughed at the girl's tricks and heard her stories, had asked to take comfort to her. Essex had seen her only seldom, and yet was concerned for her bodily and spiritual well-being. The second time he visited her, he took with him a bible, and Elizabeth had smiled gently - he had such faith in the innate goodness of even such a mean, ill-raised creature.

She composed herself now to deal gently with the girl if she were penitent, yet not to yield too much.

"Highness," the girl said. "I have thought on this long and hard, and only one thing I can think to tell you. When you were small, did you ever shake small fingers with someone to end a quarrel?"

Elizabeth frowned and shook her head.

"Perhaps it is not done among nobles. It means this, Highness - whatever quarrel is between us, to save your life, I would lose one of my small fingers. It means the quarrel is not over, but it is not bigger than our friendship, you see? Sometimes it ends the quarrel, sometimes it just takes a piece of the sting from it. The quarrel between us - I don't know that I even understand what it is, or if there is any way I can end it, short of being false to you, and that I will not. But I will say this, meanwhile. To save your life - I would lose one of my small fingers."

"That is a small thing indeed. A thumb, or long finger - I could see you would miss that. But what is a small finger? Or the promise of it."

"Highness - if it is such a small thing, a knife lies just there, beside the fruit. You could cut off your own small finger, to show me how small a thing I offer."

And there it was. Spite dressed as penitence.

Elizabeth smiled gently, and shook her head. "I think - I think you have been long enough hemmed in. You're right - the quarrel between us is not over. Yet while I deliberate on your behaviour, you should have again the freedom of the palace. I was mistaken to think to teach you anything by leaving you to solitary thought."

Elizabeth shook her head very faintly to rid herself of unwelcome thoughts, and devoted her attention again to the Italian prelate. He was explaining something of the gifts of his scrawny, young companion, gifts that had proved a diversion to many of the crowned heads of Europe, and which were a constant source of delight to his Exaltation the Pope. Gifts which Archbishop Parker - here Archbishop Parker nodded, allowing his agreement - had admired, notwithstanding the doctrinal differences which existed between the Catholic Mother church, and the infant British creation (Archbishop Parker frowned becomingly, with precisely the right glint of self-mockery).

Gifts which would probably not distract her from the minor, vexing difficulty that Elizabeth experienced when Dudley spent seemingly every waking moment with the noxious creature, as Elizabeth had come privately to refer to the girl in the privacy of her own mind.

He had asked her if she minded him spending time in the girl's company, and she had dismissed the notion airily, determined that he should realise on his own account, had he the wit, that the girl's company was undesirable. Was he incapable of seeing what was so obvious to Elizabeth?

Elizabeth excused herself absently from the company of the Italian prelate, and glanced apologetically at his companion, and at Archbishop Parker. Making her way from the room, refusing all offers of company, a small part of her mind concerned itself with identifying the expression on the Italian prelate's companion's face. Not disappointed; not offended. Relieved? Grateful? Perhaps his gifts were not then so great, or at least not reliably great.

Another, larger part of her mind was becoming aware that she was leaving this place, where she could move neither forward, nor back, nor to this side, nor to that side. Soon she would know where she must go, and soon she would have to go there.

The courtiers she had left would now be explaining to the honoured guests that Elizabeth was, now and again, prone to migraine, and must seek solitary comfort, whatever the demands of her court.

Kempe would be jealous, believing Elizabeth was now seeking the comfort of the noxious girl's clever hands, where once it was Kempe's tisanes and soothing voice that were her only small hope.

And now her feet had brought her quietly through her garden - her own garden - to a place where she could, unobserved, hear all that was said in the bower, and she must now still her mind and listen.

"No. It is not my destiny to be taken to your mother's house, and for her to learn to love me. Even for you, I will not turn aside from my destiny - it has cost too much."

His voice was quieter than hers, so quietly pleading that Elizabeth couldn't distinguish the words of his plea.

"I would tell you my destiny if I knew it. It seems that I can say only what it is not. I thought that I was to be her sister. Even when it was clear she could not be my sister, I thought I could still be hers, be kind to her, speak truth to her. But I can no more speak truth to her than I could speak it to Somerset. The words leave my mouth, and turn in the air, and when they enter her ear they have become something altogether different."

Dudley said something quiet, reassuring now, comforting rather than pleading.

"It's not that she is cruel to me it's not that I suffer here. It's not that she has me beaten by a woman who hates me, it's not that she has taken from me the only things I could bring from my home, that even Somerset gave me leave to keep."

Something large began to turn over within Elizabeth's mind, some sleeping leviathan which, woken, would displace oceans and wreck cities.

"What it is - " The girl paused, seeking the right words. Elizabeth found she was holding her breath, and made herself breathe, steadily, shallow. "The first time you spoke to me, the first thing you asked me - do you remember?"

Elizabeth leaned closer, listened as hard as she could, but could make out only a thoughtful silence, followed by a three syllable murmur, a fleeting endearment.

"Yes! And she has never, all the time I have been here, she has never asked my name. 'Girl' she call me, always. She is not like Somerset, I swear she's not. Yet she look at me just how he looked at me. I think he knew my mother's name - he never used it, though. He liked us better nameless, it made us more useful to him. Dudley - what am I to do? I cannot serve my destiny, and I cannot run from it neither. What can I do?"

Elizabeth backed out of her listening place, careful to displace no twig, no leaf, and let her feet return her to her room, where Kempe waited, grateful and concerned, ready to soothe or serve her. She could ask nothing, only reach for the book, the roughly bound book with the childish writing in the spaces between the print.

Someone's secret, but she couldn't remember whose, or where -
Lot's daughters, that she remembered. She turned there impatiently,
and puzzled over the large 'R' in the margin, and the line under Moab.

It told her nothing. For comfort alone, she leafed onwards, to Ruth
and Naomi, emblems of faith and friendship, and there she found it. A
line under Moabitess, and in the great space left over after the begats,
in that same childish script, 'R a blessing to the world - so God blessed
L's daughters' intent, and did not curse their sin'

Knowing now what she would find, she leafed her way to the
front. Her brother's bible, indeed, that had found its way into the
hands of - of one who cherished it, who learned it well, and not by rote
alone.

Elizabeth found her way to the chair before her mirror. The
leviathan began to wake, the image in her mirror, pinched and pale,
eloquently telling her how much pain she would suffer in its grip.

Her father had always seen only what touched his wishes, and
believed people should have no life outside of his wishes. When had
she become so like him?

She had lived so long in dread of her sister Mary's suspicion and
hatred. How had she come to let herself be ruled by suspicion and
hatred?

She must learn from this. When she sent away .... the girl, when
she sent her away to a convent with instructions that she be treated
gently, when she sent Dudley back to his mother, for how could she
now look upon him, she must not let herself forget them and so treat
others as badly. She must find the strength to do what she must to
hold her throne, and yet not become a tyrant.

She longed to close her eyes against the pain that gripped her, but
held them open, until her image glowed like the sun. England sun or
Afric? How could she be as constantly warm as sun of Afric, when she

had known only sun of England, when she could be only England's child?

She closed her eyes, a second only, and forced them open again. Not England sun, and not Afric.

She should be the sun that shone alike on England and Africa, distant enough to see both at one time, warm enough to bless both at such a distance. That sun, she must be, that sun.

When Elizabeth roused from the stupor that came over her, she felt weak and empty, but knew herself as ready as she could be for what she now must do. She reached for Kempe and found her ready as always to lend her strength to Elizabeth's purpose. With help, she walked steadily into her audience chamber, found her place, and summoned the girl and Dudley to attend her.

The court, that had been buzzing with talk as a beehive, buzzed louder and then grew still. When the girl came to sit, stiff, in her old, accustomed place by Elizabeth's side, and Dudley to stand, stiff, facing her, the room was silent, and all eyes on the central tableau.

"Dudley," she said, her voice sounding high and false to her own ears, "I think you must know that I hold you in great affection."

Dudley made an uncertain half-bow.

Elizabeth continued, "I - I feel that whatever sentiment you feel towards me is the affection of a brother for a sister."

"I would not know - I have no sister."

From the corner of her eye, Elizabeth saw the girl lean forward slightly. Reading in the gesture a wish for Dudley to be careful, she herself began to relax.

"Then you must trust me, for I have had a brother, and loved him well. I say that you are my beloved, younger brother. You will bow to my wisdom in all matters that touch the welfare of my subjects - although your conscience, of course, remains your own - and as my brother must be well-provided, I will draw up the papers to cede you my lands in Essex. The property is among the finest I hold - I would put it second only to the lands in Kent, which are especially dear to me."

Dudley said, "Your Highness is too kind," in tones of great mistrust.

Elizabeth gestured his thanks aside.

"When you marry," she said, "Your bride will be - is - my sister. To her, on the happy day of the wedding, go my lands in Kent. They will remain hers, come what may. Goes she to a nunnery, the land goes with her."

The girl had turned, and was looking at her with disbelief.

"Highness - do you know what you have done?"

Elizabeth tilted her chin, playing petulant. "I am Queen, I will not be questioned."

She was unprepared for the flash of pure dismay that crossed the girl's face.

"There is nothing I can do to repay you," she said, "There is nothing I can give you."

Elizabeth felt empty. The pleasure she had begun to feel flattened into loneliness as pure as she had ever felt.

She looked down, then started as her wrist was taken in a fierce grip.

"Promise, Highness. Promise, if there is ever anything I can do to repay you, if it should mean my life, promise you will ask it!"

"You could -"

"Yes!"

"You could let go of my wrist."

The girl looked down as if puzzled, and then fairly threw Elizabeth's hand from her, wide-eyed with fright.

Elizabeth leaned from her chair toward the kneeling girl, tentatively reaching a hand to her. It was as tentatively taken. She smiled, and was rewarded with a smile returned.

Elizabeth looked again at Dudley.

"Make all haste to inform your family of this union, and may it be known that I would have it accomplished with all seemly haste."

Dudley was bowing his acquiescence, when Archbishop Parker strode into the small group and said, simply, "No."

He went on to speak with great calm, and great dignity. He allowed that the Protestant church was freer than the Catholic - and yet there must be limits. The marriage of a son of Adam with any class of performing animal was, must be, eternally unthinkable. Elizabeth listened, and wished to argue, but heard echoes of what had been, until hours ago, her own voice, and was made dumb by those echoes. She listened as he numbered the ways by which he would make his wishes known to all the Archbishops of England, enlisted the aid of his Italian guest, who had the ear of the Pope himself, and who therefore could confirm that, in the Catholic church as in the Protestant, such an unholy union would not, could not be countenanced.

Elizabeth listened as her plans, her great sacrifice, her new-found generosity of spirit, were made null by these two dignified adversaries.

Queen she might be - but if she wished to see her sister happily wed to the man who loved her, it seemed she must excommunicate herself both from Rome, and from her father's church, and begin a new religion consisting only of herself, Dudley, and the still-unnamed girl, in which she was, not only the supreme, but also the sole representative of God on earth.

And now, forward came the companion, entirely without dignity or grace of bearing, leaning awkwardly around Parker to even be visible to Elizabeth. Yet his voice was calm and sweet to her ears.

"Highness, permit me, please. I am ordained, not long ago, true, but still, I can speak for Peter with all necessary authority. I am also something of an expert on performing animals - having been one myself for many years now, at the behest of his Holiness the Pope." He paused here to grin briefly at the girl, disarming her beginning indignation. "If the marriage can be made with not-quite-seemly haste, it should manage to predate my excommunication, and then - your Highness permitting - it would be a great honour if I could be granted a place at your court, wherein to study, and try my memory against real things, against truth."

Elizabeth bit her lip. She wanted this man's service, so far as fulfilling her promise - but the presence of an unknown, ungainly, soon-to-be-defrocked priest with yet unknown gifts, but evident wilfulness - she could foresee that this could become an embarassment.

He read her expression accurately.

"Highness - no. I do not ask quid pro quo, I should not have embarrassed you by offering my self along with my service. I will marry these two because I believe it right, and because I do not think I can be prevented - apologies, gentlemen.

After that, I will travel, or stay - but if you will me to stay, I assure you, I will be your most honest servant."

Elizabeth smiled. "It has recently been made clear to me that an honest servant is worth - has worth," she continued, seeing a truth unfold as she spoke, "That cannot be measured by mere coin. Coin's worth being only an agreed thing," she went on, risking a sidewise glance at the girl, rewarded by her mute encouragement, "While loyalty is a real thing, not changed by time or place or circumstance. Sir I will be, I believe, as honoured to receive your service as I am to acknowledge the service of this, my sister."

He shrugged. "Then I will marry this, your sister, to this your brother - although for the first time I begin to believe that God may have some quarrel with this endeavour."

The girl laughed outright. "Fear not," she said, "For in the first part, you should know that while Elizabeth is sister to both of us, I am not his sister, and he is not my brother.

"Further, even if this marriage may be sin in the eyes of some, so we all be of pure heart and honest intent, that is what God will see."

"Think you so?"

"I know it - for Ruth was a great blessing to the world, a grandmother to the Christ-child himself, and was she not descended from Moab?"

The young man frowned, and leaned back on his heels a little. Then his face cleared, and he said

"Of course! I have never put those things together before, but you are entirely right. I look forward to many more discussions with you, I am sure we have much to teach each other."

Elizabeth wondered how it was that she, Queen after all, did not excite such fervent admiration as this girl did. She sighed, without meaning any other to hear it, yet the young priest turned to her instantly, and smiled at her so warmly that she felt both shamed and comforted.

"Highness, may I belatedly present myself. I was born Filippo Bruno - however, since my ordination, I have gone by Giordano. You may pick which you prefer to live with following my excommunication - or pick a third, if you will."

"I have no liking for the name Filippo - Giordano Bruno, however, has a certain music. I would like to introduce my sister to you - " She paused, and looked warily at the girl, who smiled, first at Elizabeth, and then at Giordano.

"My mother always called me Cat. I see no need for any other name, until you give me his," she said, glancing sidelong at Dudley, and all her mirth gone solemn.

Cat wondered what was wrong with her. She had both her destiny, and the man she had been willing to give up for it. She had met his parents, weeks after the hasty marriage, and they had been kind and welcoming. It was churlish to wonder if they'd have been equally welcoming if she'd walked into their house barefoot, and Elizabeth's enemy.

She and Elizabeth were not enemies now. Not friends - too careful yet, too wary. But some day they might be friends.

Dudley and she still gloried, wallowed in their married state. He could touch her cheek, she could turn into his embrace, and if any scowled or tutted, they were circumspect about it if Elizabeth was near.

And here was Kempe, no longer with the switch always ready, polite now, full of would you please, and if you would be so kind. A new guest to meet her, probably another of Dudley's far-flung relatives, and how could she go on being polite to them? Why did the thought of being polite to them make her want to fling herself at the floor and drum her heels on it? What was wrong with her?

She followed close on Kempe's heels, not gaining enough that the other woman could make eye contact, fighting the urge to shriek, or weep. She stopped dead as she saw who it was who waited. It could be no other, yet she looked too small, far too slight, and wary where Cat remembered a woman always bold.

Cat advanced slowly, one step at a time, until she caught her mother's eye. Her mother turned fully to face her, and looked at her, up and down, a long time. Her smooth brow was marred now, a clumsy mark, straight and shiny as a knife-blade.

Cat saw it, and bit her lip. She looked quickly across the hall, knowing to the inch where Dudley was, knowing he would see her plea and answer it, while she returned to holding her mother's gaze.

Dudley came to hold hands with her, formal as a court portrait, and Cat smiled at last.

"Mother, this is my husband. His mother and father are here somewhere - I can introduce you to them in a while. But first - first there is something I must say to you alone - away from all these people. Dudley - I am sorry, even you."

Dudley smiled.

"You've told me often how you longed to see your mother again. I thank you for thinking to introduce us before you took time to be alone with her. Think me not so weak that I cannot stand an hour in court without a prop - although in recent time, that has been said of me, I know."

Cat hurried her mother to her room, still hers, though she had now more elegant rooms with Dudley. She'd asked to keep it, as she had asked to go on working with the washerwomen, and many whispered, but Elizabeth would deny her nothing. She trembled, both with the desire to speak, and with the desire to stay silent - for if she stayed silent, her mother need never know her guilt. But Cat would - and having prayed often for the chance to ask her mother's forgiveness, she knew she must, and without delay, without even an hour's delay to lay her head in her mother's lap and speak to her of Dudley.

At last, here was her room, her mother on the one bed, Cat all in her new finery kneeling on the floor before her.

"Mother, I am sorry."

"Child, why should you be sorry? None of what happened was your doing."

"It was, though - I wanted a carriage, and a fine husband. I wished Seymour upon us."

For a moment Cat bore her mother's shocked gaze - and then, indignant, her laughter.

"It's true - even if you don't believe me. Don't laugh at me!"

"Oh, I don't misbelieve you, Cat. You got strong wishes - I see them now I know to look. But see - I got strong wishes too. Where you think you get it from? Not from your father, that's for sure. Not one of his wishes could stand straight without a pile of gold to lean on, or move an inch without an Archbishop and a bunch of soldiers behind it and pushing hard. No - my wishes were the strong ones, I always knowed that."

Cat had gathered blame to her like a child with fresh picked berries - she wasn't sure she wanted anyone else to have any.

"Are you saying you wished yourself into a bawdy house?"

"Oh, worse than that, Cat, worse by far! There's a deal of things I thought you didn't need to know - were better off not knowing. I never told you why I came to England in the first place."

Cat frowned. "You did! You told me you were sold - you and your mother."

"True. But I didn't tell you why I wished it on us."

Now Cat was shocked. "Why would you wish such a thing?"

"Long story. Settle, now and listen.

"When I was small, I envied my older sister. I saw my Ama and Aba laying aside jewels for her, and I envied her sore.

"Ama and Aba told me my day would come for jewels - but seeing what they had stacked up for their first daughter, I couldn't believe there would be a gem left in the world when it came my turn.

"Day came when an old woman came by, woman I'd never seen before. That night Kela went dancing down to the river with the old woman, and our Ama, and a bunch of other women. She didn't dance back though. She walked back like she was older than the oldest of them. I was supposed to be sleeping, but I watched them go, and I watched them come back, and I sneaked to see Kela, curious to know what had happened. Knew she'd be getting all them jewels the next day, and I kind of figured that until she had them, we was still even. Was I ever wrong.

"She let me know what had happened. Showed it to me."

Cat chewed her lip. This wasn't one of her mother's better stories about back home. There was no good food in it, no warm sun, no dancing to speak of so far, not real dancing. And now the story had gone quiet.

Her mother started to speak again, slowly, carefully.

"Say, someone was to cut the tips of these fingers here. Say they was to sew what was left of the fingers down to the palm of your hand right here."

Cat swallowed back on bitter sourness. "They did that to her?"

"Child, no. That's only what it was worse than. See, you got two hands. If they did that to one hand, you'd still have the use of the other."

Cat shook her head, not understanding, but didn't ask the question that would make her mother answer more fully.

"Soon as I saw it, my wishes bounced right the other way. She was welcome to all the jewels in the world, I didn't want one of them, should that be how they were paid for. From that day, when I rose up in the morning, I wished that would never happen to me, and when I lay down at night, I wished it again.

"Years later, I was seeing a little pile of pretty things growing, each time my Aba came home, and I was being patted and caressed, and told how big I was growing. And my wishes fiercening and fiercening.

"That's when the travellers came. They had fine things, and they looked at my Ama, and they looked at me. They made an offer.

"If my Ama had mothered a boy, Aba might have kept her. If I'd been ready for betrothing, he might have been less willing to yield me up. As it was, he looked at a bride-price he'd never seen the like of, and there we were, gone. He probably had six wives before we were out of sight, and three sons on the way.

"My mother never learned their tongue. Me, I learned every tongue I came across, at least a little bit. I looked after Ama, until time came that I noticed she was laying things aside. A knife, and a candle, a needle, strong thread. A strip of leather. I could see her gathering courage, too, to do what she knew was still undone, and no old woman around who knew how to do it right.

"While she was still finding her courage, I was sent on a ship, a gift for English nobility, and my Ama stayed behind. Never saw her again.

"After that, I had the jewels I'd wished for as a child, and payed for them sweet way, not salt way.

"Sometimes, I wished my wishes had been kinder on Ama. Know what, Cat child? I think if I be sacrificed to your wishes - I think that be amends enough. Women always be sweeter to a child's child than to their own child - way of the world. Reckon she'd buy your happiness with both of ours. Reckon my wishing can rest now - yours can take over."

Cat stared at her mother a long time, waiting foolishly to be told what she should do next. She didn't understand half the story she'd been told, and didn't know what questions to ask to make it clearer.

Didn't know that she should ask for it to be made clearer until she'd thought a bit more about what she already knew. Fast learning was patchy, fast learning was dangerous.

Eventually, tentatively, she inclined her head towards her mother's lap, waiting for welcome or a pat and off-you-go. Welcome came, and she settled in, silent for a while, deciding which of the stories of Dudley she would tell first.

Cat sailed down the corridor, angry and glad of it. Her old room had somehow become her mother's, so that if she wished solitude she must seek it in some corner of the garden. But now it was not solitude she sought, but an audience - a particular audience.

Her mother sat at the end of the bed, squinting her way through a pamphlet. Her eyes were less good than they had been, and she wouldn't go to seek better light, or have a servant bring more tapers. She still tried to be unobtrusive in her needs.

"Spreadable or shareable, child?" she would ask, when Cat offered her more at dinner, more of anything. Cat would look down at the brimming dish, remembering the times she'd heard the same over one heel of bread. She knew the difference still - just found it hard to apply it as strictly. Spreadable was anything you could give and have exactly the same to give another time.

Songs and stories and kisses. Sun in summer, ice in January. Spite and slaps and curses. Shareable was anything that diminished as it was given, be it meat or poison.

"Shareable."

"Then I've had what I need, and I'll not take more."

Cat spoke as soon as she had cleared the doorway.

"That Newbury! She acts like we be friends. Like we could ever be friends."

Her mother sighed, put the pamphlet to one side, her head to the other.

"Newbury. She the one that beat you?"

"No - that was Kempe. I don't mind her - she's polite to me, I'm polite to her, neither of us seek out the other. Newbury's young and pretty. Hasn't found a man yet, and full of questions about me and Dudley, and when I growed up, and dying to tell me of her mother and her family."

"Tchah, to think. Tell Elizabeth that - maybe she chop her head off for you."

"That's not funny."

Her mother sighed again. "She never beat you?"

"No. But she never spoke for me when Kempe beat me."

"How you know that - did you watch her night and day? Maybe she spoke for you when you not around for Kempe to be slighted in front of - or for Elizabeth to be riled up more by."

"I never heard her speak for me."

"Did you hear her speak against you ever?"

"No."

This wasn't going the way Cat had planned it.

"Did she ask about your home and your family, and talk about hers, when you first came here?"

"Yes," said Cat grudgingly, "But why not? It cost her nothing."

"And what would it cost you now to answer her questions and ask for her stories?"

"You don't understand," said Cat.

"True. Maybe you should try to explain it so I can understand."

"All her stories - they are all how she played with her brothers, and how her father denied her nothing, and her mother would scold her because she didn't treat her good things well enough."

"She bores you? Fine, don't listen. But why be angry at her?"

"No! She has never - " she paused, re-gathered her thoughts. "Kempe, Kempe was afraid when Mary suspected Elizabeth, and Elizabeth herself lost her mother when she was tiny, and her father hot and cold with her. Newbury has never known a moment's fear, never lost anything. Her favourite pony was sent with her when she came here. How can I talk to her?"

Her mother looked at her a long moment.

"She has never hurt you?"

"No."

"Have you seen her hurt this pony of hers?"

"No. She cares for it well enough - although the hard work is always for someone else to do."

"She must find a husband, must she not?"

"And so she needs white hands, I know. How can I talk to her? Why should I talk to her? She knows nothing of real life."

"Real life? A father who loved her, a mother who loved her - she made them up, did she?"

Cat stayed silent, knowing herself in a corner already. She knew the latitude and longitude, and height and depth of her mother's world. Was this real or not real, or that strange equatorial thing 'agreed'? Was this spreadable or shareable? Was this good or bad? She was busy putting Newbury into the right place in this world, and Cat, who would not lie, would be the source of all her knowledge. Sometimes, she wished the woman would just listen, and not be always weighing and judging.

"Has she ever taken anything that was rightly someone else's? Does she put her wants over the needs of others?"

Cat stayed silent, but knew her mother could read her silences as well as her speech, good light or bad. Truth was, in the days when Cat had lectured Elizabeth, her mother's words pouring easy out of her mouth alongside her own, Newbury had taken each word to heart, tried herself against it as Elizabeth had first resisted. In some ways, Cat knew, Newbury was harder on herself, kinder to others than Cat herself. She had said once, "I know I'm lucky. I know I've had more than my share already. What can I do, but try to be good?"

The reason Cat knew Newbury had never spoken for her was because Newbury herself, weeping, had explained that she would not. She was sent to court to prepare the way for her brothers. To do that, she must court Elizabeth. She loved Cat as a sister - but had been raised all her life to know that brothers came first. She had asked Cat's pardon, and since Cat had never seen other than sorrow in Newbury's eyes when Elizabeth had one of her white rages on her, and since she had always left the room, or looked away when Kempe picked up the switch, Cat had granted it. Had honestly believed she granted it. But now Newbury's relief, and Newbury's joy, Newbury's bound determination to make up for lost time - they all grated.

Cat tried one more time to make her mother understand.

"If she had ever lost anything - if she had suffered, really suffered, for even a day -"

She fell silent, not liking her mother's look, uneasy herself that she had come close to ill-wishing the girl, never meaning to.

"I wish her no harm, I wish her happiness," she said swiftly. "But how can I talk to her?"

Her mother sighed. "You've chosen a narrow path there. It's true that wide roads can lead to bad places. But do not mistake the truth, child. There are narrow paths that lead to bad places also."

"And that's the kind of path I've chosen?"

"Maybe. Maybe not."

She was silent for long moments, and Cat began to think she would not speak again, but finally she said, slowly, "There are people in the world, you know, who've suffered more than you have. I been hard on you sometimes, made you outwork your strength, but I always loved you - you know that?"

"Yes - I know that."

"Some children in this world don't got a mother for no time at all - or worse, got a mother who hate them. That happened many times in this world, you know, and I see no way to stop it happening again."

"I know that!"

"So. There be three kinds of people, yes? People more lucky than you - that be Newbury, yes? People as lucky as you - shall we say Kempe, or Elizabeth?

"And then we have people, not small number of people neither, looking at you when you with your Dudley, we have people less lucky than you. And out of all those people, seems you can only be friends with them middle ones, the Kempes and the Elizabeths. And not even all of them, for I think Kempe be not your friend, and you not hers."

Cat found her voice at last, indignant. "Why would I not be friends with people less lucky than me? You don't think I would spurn them?"

"But child - surely they must spurn you?"

She sat silent for a moment, while Cat turned that over, and then smiled, a smile Cat had not seen in years, the smile of a lioness with the prey finally boxed in beyond question.

"Unless, they be more generous of spirit than you - in spite of they lack of advantages."

Cat opened her mouth to spring to her own defense - and closed it again, over words unspoken that she knew would be no help.

"You," she said finally, "You are so..."

"I know child - I know."

Cat leaned against her, twice as angry as when she came in, twice as glad. "Stone comfort," she murmured, pushing in against her mother without any move to embrace.

"Bone comfort," her mother murmured back, wrapping arms around the sodden lump that was Cat, and for a moment, they were again the Only Two, learning together how to love each other in good times and bad, in times of anger and disagreement and hanging boredom.

Cat walked through the garden, letting herself think a thing that she had spent a long while carefully not thinking. Newbury had never spoken for Cat - but Cat had seen her grow suddenly clumsy as Elizabeth was winding herself into a hot rage - and whether it ended in laughter or scolding, still the white rage didn't happen that day.

Newbury was sitting in the arbour, looking a little sad. As Cat approached her she looked up, warily, not welcomingly. Cat sat beside her.

"My mother thinks I've been unfair to you."

"Oh?"

"I think it's loathsome that a woman should be right all the time. Couldn't she practice to be wrong, just for once, just to be a little agreeable?"

"That sounds unlike any mother I know. And not true to the high ideal of motherhood. You should wash out your mouth. Shall I come and watch?"

Cat twitched her nose at Newbury.

"All right, I have a better idea. Since we are now two, we can go to visit the Signor. Elizabeth asked me to go earlier, but have you noticed? Either alone can be amusing - together, they're deadly. Ponderous questions of religion or politics, and long silences, empty but for the grinding of mighty intellects. I fall asleep just thinking of it.

"And think! I said 'No' to Elizabeth. She's grown so humble, I forget myself. And she did not press the point at all. Kempe looked me daggers, though. Perhaps because I showed such disrespect to Highness - perhaps because it meant she must go in my place."

They had risen together, and made their way to the Signor's door, arms twined together, comfortable again. The Signor's door was open, and so Cat tapped it gently and let it swing open.

"Ladies!" he exclaimed, "Come in - let me speak to you. I have learned something wondrous. And not in my journeyings abroad, but in the very kitchen of the palace. You were right, beauteous Cat, to lead me to people who work - but sit, sit and I will tell you."

Cat and Newbury looked around, found a small space of table untroubled by books or found things, and leaned up against it, composing themselves in a parody of comfort.

Bruno placed one hand dramatically on his own head. "The first thing," he said, "You place here, upon your head."

Cat nodded accommodatingly, "And the second on the lid of my eye, and the third on the end of my nose. Mouth, ear, shoulder, hand, navel, knee, foot," she said, gesturing to each in turn, to reassure him that she would scrupulously memorise the things he told her, then settled expectantly for his promised glimpse of something rich and strange.

Bruno did not continue, but only looked at her - Newbury, too, she found looked strangely at her. As the silence grew, Cat found a surprisingly fierce thing looking at her from Bruno's mild eyes.

"The first time we met - did I not tell you to speak to me of every single thing you knew? And how many times have we met since then?"

Cat edged even closer to Newbury. "This?" she asked, patting the top of her own head. "That's not something I know. It - it's how I know things. Doesn't everyone so?"

Bruno shed his ferocity like a coat, revealing his usual air of wonderment. Cat and Newbury exchanged glances, relieved, and fully as entertained as they had hoped to be.

"I see - like you would not tell me that you know how to read, or how to arrange your hair - it was, to you, a thing expected. And yet, until I spoke to Signor the Cook, I had never known that there was a second Art of Memory, completely unlike the one I was raised to."

"An Art of Memory?" said Cat, honestly puzzled. "No - there's no art. No castles or cathedrals. Just, here is your head, and put something on it. It's work, not art."

"But isn't there more? Signor the Cook said that there was more, but that he could not speak of it yet. Yet he seemed not more busy then than he had been. I think perhaps my ear failed me - it has not been long enough among the English."

"Oh, that's because you must learn your own body before you can take another."

Now Newbury looked at her as if she was slowly growing horns, and the fierce thing that had looked from Signor Bruno's eyes was back. Cat hastened to speak on, "But, of course, since you have long studied the true Art of Memory, I think it would be for you to decide if you want to know the next step of this small thing."

"Speak," said Signor Bruno, with none of his usual circumlocutions.

"Well - first thing is, you would usually be small when you start, and you'd start with just your head, and when you always could trust one thing, you'd then try the next. You'd be a lot bigger by time your Mother started to speak of animals to you, and that would be when you had need. First animal you pick is one you like best, and really comfortable with. Won't work if you scared at all."

She waited. Bruno waited. Finally he said, impatiently, "I suppose - Bruschetta, my horse. She's the only animal I've known for long, and she's kind enough."

"All right. But before the next part, you have to go ask her permission. If she say no, you have to find another."

He looked at her. She looked back. She knew she had the edge over him, and need do nothing but wait and be quiet. Finally he left.

Cat smiled and flounced her skirts, well pleased with herself. It was almost the best thing in the world, to explain something that you knew, and that another lacked. She looked round to Newbury, who seemed drawn into herself. Well, it was probably a mistake to think things between them were mended so easily. The will was there on both sides - now a little time, a little patience was also needed.

Bruno returned. "She gave - well, she did not withold her permission. I would say she raised no objection to assisting me in this journey - although I think she would prefer a real road beneath us."

"Then, the next time you have a set of ten things to remember, you do as Cook told you - but first, you close your eyes, and in your mind you become Bruschetta. And then, for a long time, you should be only sometimes you, sometimes the horse, and once you are ready, you can choose other animals. They should all be different from you, and from Bruschetta, and from each other.

"You could have, let's say, Bruschetta for things of the intellect. For - people who owe you money, you might have a cow, maybe. You see?"

"I think I see. And this is all of it?"

"Almost all. The last part only works if all of your animals are devoted to one kind of knowledge. Let us say Signor the Cook is planning a big feast. He needs all of his animals, lined up in a row so he can plan the work, and count amounts, and so on. Now, comes Highness to ask for one more thing, a simple thing, it will not really work for something complicated. All of Cook's animals are busy already - yet all of the ingredients Cook needs for the new dish are also there. Then he could make a rhyme - eye of cat, toe of mouse, ear of bat - it will really only work for a novelty - but then Highness, she does love her novelties."

Bruno was silent a moment, telling something over in his head.

"And you learned this all of this from your mother?"

"First from my mother - but even before we were parted, we worked differently. Eventually, yourself is the only one that can teach you."

"I would speak with your mother also, about her way of learning."

Cat shrugged. "I will bring her to you."

"No!" he said, and then thought for a moment. "If I speak to you both together, you will both give me half a story. Better you come to me with one companion, and she with another. That way I will get two stories."

Cat knew that this was not all the truth, if it was truth at all. There was something a little sly looking out of the Signor's candid eyes. She turned over in her mind the possible reasons a man could have to want to see mother and daughter always separately, and could not like any of them.

Bruno spoke again. "And now - now I must give my mind to it. Put the stick across the window as you leave."

And that was that. Cat glanced a laugh at Newbury - which was not returned by her - and as they left, Cat picked up the stick that lay beside the path, and propped it across the corner of his window. Now, the only visitor that would pass his door would be one bringing food, or bearing away old crocks, and they would not exchange words with him.

Cat turned, and tried to link arms again with Newbury, but Newbury stood deliberately away from her.

"You are a dabbler in witchcraft," she said coldly.

Cat straightened. "I dabble in nothing," she said. "Witchcraft is an old and simple thing - look at the words. Witch is knowledge - craft is work. I no more dabble in witchcraft than I dabble in reading - both are second nature to me."

She might as well not have spoken.

"And the Signor - a man of God! I watched you explain to him how he should take a familiar. He may not have known what he was hearing, but I did."

"Think, Newbury! Familiar means well-known - that's all. If you want to give your mind to learning new things, the means by which you do it must be as well known to you as your own body, or the body of a beloved animal. Your pony -"

"Fah! Speak no further, I will not hear you," said Newbury, and she sped along the path as if devils followed her, rather than one bewildered girl.

The worst part of it was, Cat knew she had earned Newbury's enmity. Not by knowing a thing, and sharing her knowledge with Signor Bruno - but by believing herself happy, and hiding her bitter confusion from Highness, and from Dudley, and even, a little, from herself. The only relief her confusion had found was dropping Newbury, letting her fall ever a little further, and a little further. And now she had turned to take Newbury up again, and it was not so easy.

Cat crept into her mother's room, not sure of what she would say, or how she would say it. She resolved to start with what she was most sure of, and carry on as best she could.

"Signor Bruno would like to meet you. He says he would like to speak to you about - well, that thing some people call witchcraft. You know - for remembering things?"

"I know. He says that is what he would like?"

"He wants not to see the two of us together. He wants more than he speaks of, but I don't know what. After where you've been, I suppose it's laughable to worry about the Signor," said Cat, feeling altogether foolish.

"Nowhere in the world is entirely safe. And no person, neither. I am grateful that you tell me this, and when I go to him, it will be with someone who wishes me well, and has enough power to make their wishes felt."

Cat smiled, relieved that her mother didn't think her foolish.

"You seem sad," her mother continued.

"Sad. And foolish," Cat said, wanting at least to be first to say it.

"Oh?"

"After I talked to you I realised I did want to be friends with Newbury. I remembered that we had been friends, true friends I think. But it seems I took her dancing over the void, and let go her hand. Not so easy to take it up again. She called me a witch."

"Well, all it means is 'knowing one'."

"Not when it's said that way."

"That's true. And we both know that's not all that's true of you. You in a strong place, and not only what you know got you there. Your Newbury can see that as well as us."

Cat could find no more to say. She stayed a while with her mother, and when she returned to her rooms with Dudley she went swiftly, wishing to see no one on the way.

The next morning, she felt brave enough to seek Newbury out. She must know where things stood, so that she could begin to distance herself from her loved ones, should that be needed.

"Have you spoken to Highness?" she asked, not wanting to be subtle.

Newbury looked down, and shook her head. Cat took a deep breath, and released it all.

Newbury looked at her a little. "She's never yet burned anyone. It seemed that with Elizabeth on the throne, the burnings were done with."

Cat nodded. "Be a shame if she started with me."

"But we are not friends," said Newbury.

"I didn't think so. And it is the only sorrow in my life."

Newbury seemed ready to speak again, then shivered, and walked quickly away. Cat watched her go, remembering how it had been to watch words twist in the air between her and Elizabeth. Now, Elizabeth trusted her more than any - and yet was out of reach. Cat loved her too much to rub her happiness against any of Elizabeth's wounds that might still be raw. And Newbury, gentle, funny Newbury feared for her own soul while Cat was near.

That evening, she spoke to Dudley.

"Would it please you to make a visit with me? To Signor Bruno? I could go alone - I am married, after all - but I wish to walk carefully. And I wish very much to speak with him."

She watched Dudley closely, and saw him discard the notion of asking after Newbury, since Cat had not mentioned her. They were both agreed that Elizabeth deserved some respite from their constant devotion to each other.

"It would please me greatly. Like all men in the court, I live in a constant fever of curiosity about the Signor."

Cat laughed.

"No, truthfully. The women of the court are always beating down his door - or moaning and sighing because he will admit no visitors. Italians, of course, are legendary - yet he seems so unprepossessing. A small carrot of a man. We are puzzled."

Cat laughed again.

"You mean, the men of the court think we visit the Signor to flatter him, and flap our eyes at him? That's not how it is."

"No?"

"No! He speaks to us of science and history. And we talk back, and - this is the thrilling part - he listens to what we say, rather than commenting on how prettily our lips move, and how the sound of our voice is like to birds in the heavens, or angels come to earth."

"Truly?"

"Truly."

"Perhaps I'll not come then, for that sounds exceeding dull."

Cat reached behind her for a beautifully patterned cushion, and delivered it straight to Dudley's head.

An hour later, the two were following the path to Signor Bruno's door, and glad to see that Signor's stick lay beside the path.

"Ah! My mistress comes, I look forward to instruction!" Bruno exclaimed, then caught the horrified glance Cat made towards Dudley.

"I am sorry - a poor joke."

"No apology needed - my humour is lacking, I am afraid. Newbury fears me, and I am troubled thereby."

"Newbury? Why does she fear you? She seemed easy enough with you when last you were here."

"That was the beginning of the trouble. What I taught you - there are some who think it is against God, that the Bible speaks against it."

"Thou shalt not suffer a witch to live."

"You have it! Although it does not say there what it is that makes one a witch and another a wise one. Newbury thinks that it is a known thing, though, and that by confiding memories to God's creatures, I am doing some harm to God. Perhaps I should cease instructing you, and instead learn the classical art of memory from you. It might be safer - and yet, I don't know that I could. It is hard to keep ones thoughts from moving in a practiced direction - I'm not sure that it can be done."

"I know that it cannot. Believe me - I have tried it, and to save my own skin, I could not do it."

"Indeed?" drawled Dudley. "And yet you live." Cat looked at him, surprised by his tone, but Bruno seemed untroubled, and answered him willingly.

"Here, I live. Believe that I married the two of you because, in my heart, I knew it to be right - I saw how you looked at each other. Believe also that had my progression through Europe made its promised end, back again in Rome, I would not long have survived my return. My confessor, in Rome, prevailed upon me to cease using the stars as a memory space. I managed this, with great difficulty, until my journey began - and then, such a flood of new ideas, I must use all of my memory places, even those forbidden. On my return to Rome, I would be imprisoned for this - and I have reason to believe I would burn before many had questioned me. My confessor named me heretic, and feared the spread of heresy - only Papo's affection for me sent me on this journey, to find friends for the Church, and to find my way back to the path of righteousness."

"And of course, you could not lie to your confessor."

Cat frowned, hearing a silken tone in Dudley's voice that did not become him.

"On the contrary - I could, and easily. But it would win me nothing worth having."

Cat cried out, "Your life, Signor! That is not worthless!"

Bruno frowned. "This is hard to explain. The only explanation I can think of - that you might comprehend - would require me to break a confidence. Neither of you plan to become stone-masons, do you?"

Cat laughed at the jump in his discourse.

"No, truthfully, as foolish as it may seem, before I can speak further, I must know that you will make no use of what I tell you, that there will be no ill consequences for one who spoke freely to me."

"For myself, I swear that I have no intent to become a stone-mason."

"I, also, so swear. I am made for fighting or courtliness - these are not the hands of one destined for dull toil."

"Well. There is a stone - fine, golden in colour, most attractive. There is no need to name it, better I leave it unnamed. What you must know about it, is this: the face the rock showed to the world while still uncarved, it must also show to the world when it has become part of a palace, or cathedral. If the block is tilted, so," and his hands described the bottom-most part of the block coming to the front, "rain, ice and sun will find a milliard tiny flaws in the rock, and in fifty years or less, it will be pocked and ugly. Fifty years more, and it must be replaced, at whatever expense, and whatever its place in the structure. The two faces look identical to the eye - yet one will face sun and ice a thousand years, and one for not even a hundred.

"I spoke to a group of masons, and the one who spoke told me that before a block was taken from the quarry, its face was marked with chalk - and this was the face that must be shown to the world for always. Later, another took me aside and explained that his craft had secrets - and yet, he felt uneasy at hearing one of his own lie to a man of the cloth. Even so small a lie - he said that a face marked with chalk was worthless - the chalk would rub off before the block had been carted ten miles. The block must be marked with ink, or pitch - something that would not rub off, no matter how it was handled."

Cat frowned. "Yet, if its beautiful golden face was marked with pitch - ah!"

Dudley said easily, "No doubt they had some means to dissolve the pitch when it had served its purpose."

"Or," Cat said triumphantly, "They marked all of the faces that must not show. Then it matters not how the stone was marked - the true face is the bare one."

Bruno grinned at her triumph - Dudley stood a little back on his heels, but smiled gamely enough when she looked to him.

"I see not the purpose of your story," he said, "Cat, perhaps you will explain it to me?"

"I see no more than you. Signor Bruno, say on?"

"You know the outline of the classical art of memory - a room will have five or ten places in it, all different: it is interesting that both arts seize upon fives and tens, I think it is more than just finger-counting, but that is not the meat of my tale. One is encouraged to use cathedrals for matters spiritual, forts for matters military, and so forth. Each thing remembered is placed in turn, and found again where it is placed, as needed. I have been encouraged, since my gift became apparent, to add continually to the structures in my mind - and yet, to use them only for fripperies. I spoke truly when I named myself a performing animal, for all I hungered after true things.

"Here is the heart of the thing. For years, I kept two structures in my mind - one for things true, or useful, or both - one for use in reciting a thousand unrelated words, or a hundred notes of not-music, whatever might catch Papo's fancy. Yet they would not remain separate. I had recourse to the twelve mansions of the Zodiac - the teacher who told me it was forbidden knew less of the art than me; I believed - still do believe - that if God keeps famine in the house of Aries, and I keep the teachings of Aristotle there, the two will never touch, any more than the writings of Ovid would have any conceivable effect on my aged teacher's psalms were we both to commit the same altar to our memory, where he would place David, and I the Ars Amatoria. You see?"

"Not remotely," Cat said, ruefully, and grinned unabashed at Dudley's look of frank relief.

Bruno paced a moment, muttering to himself. Dudley seemed apprehensive, Cat had seen the same thing too often before to be troubled by it.

"It is like this," Bruno said finally. "Everything in my mind, palaces, forts, cathedrals, the heavens themselves - they join together. They are forever separate from those same palaces, forts, cathedrals in the mind of any other - even God himself, if we admit of such a being - but in my mind, nothing is truly separate from anything else. It follows, then, that I must dwell, at all times, on the poor man's proverb - you know it? That it is hard to tell a single lie. One lie begets another, there is no way to prevent it. I wish to give my life to the knowledge of true things - and therefore should shun all things meaningless, and more than things meaningless, should dread things false. Each stone in each place in my mind, palace or garden wall or shepherd's hut, must be well-placed, and nothing to mark it with but my own wit. No part of my wit can be given to maintaining a lie, even one that would buy me twice the life I've had already. To do what with? Eat bread and beat my head against any wall I could reach? Fah," he exclaimed, and was still.

"So, knowledge is your only mistress," said Dudley into the silence. Cat turned on him - from Bruno, such leaps were to be expected, but not from Dudley.

Bruno sighed. "I know what it is you wish to know," he said.

"Do you so?" asked Dudley, and Cat turned her gaze first on one, then on the other, unable to fathom this new turn to the conversation, but willing to let it play out before she asked the question that burned in her own mind.

"Your wife, your beautiful bride, could have come alone to my door, as any married woman can, according to custom here. And you cannot help but wonder - if she had come alone, would we now be sitting at opposite ends of this room, speaking only of truth and falsehood, and the secrets of stone-masons."

Cat stretched her eyes wide, and turned on Dudley, who would not look at her.

"I will say this, and hope that it contents you. I joined your hands in marriage, and never saw I two more rightly joined. My eye finds great beauty in your wife - but only the beauty of a painting admired from afar. I have no itch to handle, or possess.

"If I could come between you, believe that I would not. If I would come between you, I know that I could not."

Dudley smiled thankfully, and Cat found her anger dissolving into curiosity. At the heart of Bruno's pretty web of words was a space, a small blank space where a single question remained carefully unanswered.

She contemplated her linked hands, then said, "So, the classical art of memory has the same risks as my own. It would seem we have neither of us any recourse but prayer."

"And one of us, not even that," said Bruno wryly.

"You do not pray?" she asked.

"I cannot. There is room in my mind only for things known. God is not known to me. I am grateful to you for telling me how money is a thing agreed: to me, God is also a thing agreed. He changes with place, and tongue, and circumstance."

"What people say of Him changes! He does not!"

"What people say of Him is all I know of Him. He does not deign to speak to me, as He clearly does to you."

Cat felt herself bereft. She had believed herself married in truth, by a man of God. It seemed now, that the only man willing to marry her to her Dudley, was one who believed himself Godless.

"Could you not believe what I say of Him?"

"Believe me - a thousand times, I would rather believe you, than such a one as Parker. But that is personal taste alone - there is no room for that in the structure I am trying to build. Will you still come and speak with me?"

His tone was light enough that she saw how afraid he was.

"Never alone," she said, it being the best that she could offer him from the shaky place that she stood.

"That is both wise, and kind," he said. "Now, answer me this. Have you left me, even once, that I have not asked you to place the stick across the window as you go?"

"Not once," said Cat, thinking over all the times she had been here.

"Then this will be no exception, and you may consider yourself most highly complimented," said Bruno, turning from both her and Dudley.

As she placed the stick across the window, she could feel Dudley's eyes on her. She turned to meet his gaze.

"I am sorry," he said, "I know I should have trusted you."

Cat stepped closer to him, so that she looked into his eyes from a very small distance away.

"I understand," she said. "It is like having a ruby in your pocket. You know it has not fallen, could not have fallen, but as you walk a street with pickpockets, it is hard to know whether to hold it tightly, or ignore it altogether - and half-measures are unwise."

Dudley reached to touch her cheek, "You are truly not angry?"

"I am truly not angry. It will be no hardship to go always accompanied into Bruno's household. It would be," she said, tentatively, "a hardship to avoid his household altogether."

He linked hands with her, and drew her down the path. "I think," he said, "that if nothing presses me, I would be always pleased to be your chaperon into the Signor's household. Would that suit?"

"You wouldn't find it burdensome?"

"I would not. In general company, he says little of note - much of what he says seems obscure and tedious. I see why, now."

"You do?" Cat asked.

"The man feels the kindling around his ankles. In his own home, he is careful whose company he invites, and then free to speak whatever comes to his mind. Where he has not chosen the company, he cannot then speak freely, and masks his true thoughts with platitudes or cryptic nothings."

Cat looked at him admiringly, pleased at his insight, forgiving herself for her brief disappointment when he failed to solve Bruno's puzzle. She laced her fingers into his, knowing that there were those in the palace who would be shocked, knowing also that a jaded courtier's shock at a couple four months married being still absorbed in each other would make them glow for each other all the more. For the world to be shocked, and God content with her - ah, that was very bliss.

Her curiosity stirred a little. Dudley was happy to escort her to Bruno, knowing that he was friend alone. Would he be as happy if he knew that she felt herself led into Dudley's arms by God - that if God led her otherwise, she would grieve, but not balk?

She had never known what it was to leave a question unanswered for a whole lifetime. That would be an interesting thing to learn.

Cat paced her room, hating herself for her cowardice, but unable to shed it. Elizabeth had summoned her, to speak to her alone. Her words - her fine, brave words, were coming back to haunt her.

'Promise you will ask it.'

Her life she would give, willingly. Dudley? Never.

She would die first, kill first, even Elizabeth, who had given her everything.

She saw herself for a fraud. She saw how she had kept from Elizabeth, kept Dudley from Elizabeth, not from fine feeling and a wish to save her pain. She had dreaded this day, when Elizabeth asked for the smallest share of what she had, and she clutched it to herself like a child with one sweet. She had hoped – foolish hope – that Elizabeth would forget the turn of Dudley's shoulder if she saw it less often, would lose her taste for the sound of his voice and the press of his hand. As if Cat would have lost one iota of her longing for him, however long she was kept from him.

Cat gathered herself together, walked the halls to Elizabeth's chamber, slid within, and watched, numb, as Kempe and Newbury swiftly departed. The time would come when she must say 'No' to Elizabeth, and say it clearly, and find out what came after. But she had a few moments yet.

Elizabeth was speaking. Cat forced herself to attend.

"It must stay a secret. Should we ever love openly, I would be universally hated - it would be hard to say who would hate me more, Protestants for raising a Catholic into a place of power, or Catholics for corrupting a man of God."

"A man of God?" Cat echoed, sounding stupid to her own ears.

"Signor Bruno! Cat! Are you not listening to me?"

"Signor Bruno? But he is so - odd." Cat winced, hearing what she had said, cursing herself for tossing her salvation back into the fire before it had begun to cool in her hands.

"I know,' said Elizabeth, laughing, unoffended.

"But, oh, how he looks at me. In his mind is a palace, and around the palace a great garden. And every tree, every bloom, every twig in that garden is a belief, or a preference, or a word of mine. I contradict myself, and he shows me the contradiction, and then shows me the exact place in his garden where it will be enshrined. How could I not love him? And he asks nothing from me, but a roof over his head, and food in his mouth, while he follows his puzzles. Cat, you were right to speak to everyone! He tells me such things – I never knew the world had so many small things in it. I listen to him, and I'm torn whether to think of the words, or just let his voice wash in to me. I daren't look at him while others are present – and I can't be apart from him – and I can't be alone with him. Oh, Cat!"

Cat just looked. She knew how love looked, and how it sounded, and Elizabeth's evident love for Bruno made her free again to look at Elizabeth, and hear her voice without fear.

"And yet," said Elizabeth, growing quieter, more still. "And yet, I have looked at him while others are present, and I have been much apart from him. And I have been alone with him."

"Elizabeth..." breathed Cat.

"Your mother has helped us. She has been with us – but not with us. She told me much that we could do, and the one thing that we must not do, and she stayed in one room, while we were alone in the other. Five times we have done that, five times only in many, many months. And, in my mind, in my heart, the one thing we must not do grew and grew until it was the only thing, and I must do it. Just once. Bruno tried to deny me, but he could not. I was ruthless in my submission, I was tyrannical. I was foolish. One time only. My mother tried so many times, over so many years - and so many others after her - how can God be so cruel in his wit?"

"Are you sure?" asked Cat. Long association with bawdy women, and her mother's willingness to answer all questions, meant that she knew the questions to ask. "How long since you should have seen blood? Is it weeks, or only days?"

"It is months," said Elizabeth simply. "I knew, in my heart, after only a few days - and I knew there were things your mother could do to help, and the sooner, the easier. And each day, I left asking her until the next day. I said I was foolish. What am I to do?"

Cat was silent a long time. She had been so sure that she knew what Elizabeth was going to ask, and that it was impossible, and therefore no further thought was needed. Now, there was only one thing she could think to do.

"Let's go and ask my mother," she said.

"No – I can't."

"Why not?"

"She frightens me."

"Lord, is that all? Well, that proves you're not a complete idiot, then."

Cat waited for the flash of Elizabeth's eyes, then seized her hand, this once not caring who saw, and propelled her down the corridor to her mother's room.

Cat's mother looked up, then closed her book, laid it to one side, and stood up to give a tiny bob

"Please," said Elizabeth in a strangled voice, "Please sit."

"I been expecting you,' said Cat's mother, "any day now. Won't be much longer before your gowns need letting out."

"I'm sorry," said Elizabeth after a little pause. "I did the one thing you told me I mustn't."

"If you want my help, there must be truth between us. I never told you what you mustn't do - not for me to say."

"You said - " Elizabeth stopped, embarassed in front of Cat.

"I said, if you welcome his part or his product into that one part of you, part where blood show, a baby be likely the next thing to show there. That's what I said."

"But I mustn't have a child."

"Who say? Not God, it looks like. Not you either, looks like. Anyone else - not theirs to say. You think I had a daughter because I was ignorant? Because I was stupid? See what's there, girl. I had a daughter because I would walk no path that took me away from a daughter, and not towards one."

Elizabeth looked, astonished, at Cat, who was a stranger creature than she had ever known. A girl, neither afterthought, nor disappointment, but satisfaction of a fervent wish.

She looked back again at Cat's mother. "You meant this to happen?" she asked.

"Stop insisting on being stupid!" said Cat's mother, either ignorant of her growing danger, or unfazed by it. "I told you how to do a thing, or how to avoid doing it. I could no more make you do it, than I could stop you doing it. You want a scapegoat, or you want help?"

Elizabeth laid a hand flat on her belly, and said nothing. Cat's mother hissed a sigh.

"If you wanted to lose this child, you'd have been here before now. And you wouldn't have been caring for yourself so well, these past months. Yes, I've seen - you've taken every last word of mine well to heart, you treat your body like it was your favourite animal, good plain food, clean water, steady exercise. No sweets, no spirits, small beer only, or watered wine. So - you want to birth a strong child. Then what? You want to give it to another to be raised, or have the raising of it yourself?"

Elizabeth shook her head. "It wouldn't be right -"

Cat's mother leaned forward and gripped Elizabeth's wrist, in defiance of all protocol. "I ask you what you want," she said fiercely, "Not what is right, not what is possible. What do you want?"

Elizabeth tilted her chin bravely. Her eyes brimmed with tears, but not one had spilled.

"Sometimes, ruling is not about what I want," she said.

"But if you want to rule well - be it yourself or a kingdom - you must know that one thing at all times. Answer the question in front of you, girl. What do you want?"

Tears spilled, freely now, down Elizabeth's face.

"I want to raise my child," she said. "I want to rule my kingdom well. I want to teach my child how to rule wisely. I want my child to be happy, and if it suit my child's nature, I want to leave my kingdom, whole, in the hands of my child to take care of when I am dust."

Cat's mother took her hand from Elizabeth's wrist, cupped it tenderly against her wet cheek. "That is my good chick," she said. "Now we have work to do."

"Work?" asked Elizabeth blankly.

"Yes, work. There is a path you can follow. In this time alone, in this place alone, and only for you, but it's there. We live in a time of miracles. People expect strange things - we just have to let them know what strange thing they expect next. Good thing you chose Bruno."

"Bruno? But he's a priest -"

"That don't concern us - you not looking to marry the man. For what we going to do, there is not a man I've seen in all my years suit our purpose better."

Elizabeth looked at Cat for help, found her as greatly puzzled as Elizabeth herself.

"Take Bruno - funny little stick that he is, with his carrot hair, and his skin that the sun hate. Grow his hair about a foot, and pile it on his head. Give him silk gown, and crown him with gold - what do you see?"

Cat said, "Elizabeth." Elizabeth just looked from one to the other.

"People look for a father in a child. Your father, you can see in both of you, clear as day. People look for a father in this child, all they will see is Elizabeth."

"So, am I to be this child's father?" asked Elizabeth.

"For those that will believe it, yes. For those that would believe otherwise - they will have another story. You must go to Parker, and you must tell him that you have been reading your bible, and it has struck you strange that Jesus stepfather is given whole line - and for Jesus true mother, you can see no line given. Say that you hunger, all of a sudden, to hear any word he can tell you of Mary's own mother. Say you do not know why you hunger to know this, but nevertheless, even if it lose you the respect of a man you greatly admire, still you must ask the question. Can you say all of that?"

"I think so - but why?"

"If you wish to ask that, ask it of him. Ask him a hundred questions, if you can think of them. Just answer nothing. Be very humble, and full of ignorance, and let him ask round his learned friends, and see what they will find. And pray you bear a daughter, for a son will have only a very few years.

"Now, Cat. You must go to Bruno, and ask him the meaning of one word - and that word be 'parthenian'."

"But won't Bruno know -"

"Child! Shed all thoughts of what you know, and what you think Bruno will know. We need Bruno because he has the ear of every alchemist in this city, and we need him for what all men now know of him - in particular, that he cannot lie to save his own life, and that he will chase the smallest truth like a miser chasing farthing towards a crack in the floor. If you cannot wake his curiosity about what can happen in this world, you are not the woman I think you. And it will help greatly if you can have at the back of your mind when you see him, how greatly concerned you are that you will one day turn a corner in the palace, and find Dudley holding Elizabeth hand."

Cat looked, shocked, at Elizabeth, and saw her sore affronted.

"There, that will do. Elizabeth, you go now and talk to Parker. Cat, I need you one minute more."

Elizabeth did not move. When Cat's mother looked at her again, she said quietly, "There are many girls in this situation. It seems not fair that there should be a path for me, when there is none for them."

"Path is still not certain, if that help you. Then, you can throw your child to the wolves, it will not give this path to anyone else. Or, you can save your child, and later, turn your attention to saving a few others. Can be done."

Elizabeth looked down at her linked hands. "My child's whole life would be based on a lie - whatever you say about asking questions, and stating nothing - we are trying to make people believe that this child is a miracle."

"Never child born that wasn't a miracle, whether it be miracle rejoiced in or miracle unwanted. Yours will not be the first, I would think."

Elizabeth still hadn't moved. "How do I know - how do I know that if I take this chance, I will remember to pay for it after? Now, I want greatly to help - later, if I begin to feel safe - will I remember to serve any other but me?"

"You keep your own conscience, child. Has to be so."

"Because I am queen," remarked Elizabeth quietly.

"Because you are person," Cat's mother replied, equally quietly. "And this you know - it in every law you have set to paper. Your mother would be so proud of you."

Elizabeth tilted her chin, ready to argue - then swallowed, seeing the certainty in the eyes regarding her.

Elizabeth looked once more at Cat. "Once before, I took from you what was yours by right. Think you I would do so again?"

Cat could find no answer. Elizabeth paused a small moment, then left. Cat looked an accusation at her mother.

"That was needed," her mother said, "I'd not have done it else. The two of you haven't been easy together for some time - you can't become bosom friends again yet. First, there is one other thing I need, and that is Newbury. The alchemists we have, and the priests of all persuasions. The people will follow Elizabeth if they see she truly love them, and she does. The nobles need to see one of their own continue to court her favour, and that must be Newbury. Go and talk to her now, before you find Bruno."

Cat knew the truth of what her mother said - but she feared to approach Newbury. Almost, she wanted to call Elizabeth back, and give her this task, but she knew that Newbury must be all won, or all lost, and Elizabeth could not win back what Cat herself had lost.

Cat went first to the chapel, and found a quiet corner, and composed herself to pray, as she often did now. She spoke silently, but fervently, fearing the strength of her own will if it be not submitted to the Lord's will.

"Lord, if it be Thy will, save Elizabeth's child. If it be Thy will, let me win Newbury back, and let me find the right words to kindle Bruno's curiosity. Lord, Thy will be done - I take nothing but at Thy hand."

She stood, and all but walked into Newbury.

"What were you praying to?" asked Newbury coldly.

"Lord God Almighty, who gave His son to save us both. Who else would I pray to in this place?"

"How would I know?"

"Newbury - I swear to you, I believe in my heart that God does not mind what I do in my head. He gave me my wits, He wills me to use them, I know it. Have you heard why Bruno cannot return to Italy?"

"Yes, I have heard. Do you believe in your heart that God loves also what Bruno does in his mind?"

"How can it hurt God, to have a little stick of a man - or a small stick of a woman - think one thing, or another? God is not so feeble."

"You know, you said you would not try to convince me."

"That was before Elizabeth had need of us."

"Elizabeth?"

The door at that point opened, and Cat bowed her head, made her last respects, and walked out, hoping that Newbury would follow her to some more private place.

She reached her rooms, and turned to find Newbury a careful pace away from her. She opened the door, and held it from the other side, waiting until Newbury was well past before stepping to close it.

"Elizabeth is with child," she said, without preamble.

"What? How?"

"Bruno. While you were with them, that was not the grinding of mighty intellects that you heard."

For only a moment, pure mischief looked back from Newbury's eyes - and then was gone.

"What will she do?"

"My mother has a plan. You may think it blasphemous, and if you do, we are lost. If you flee Elizabeth's side, the web we spin is ripped in one small space, and then the great weight it holds will bring it down."

"Tell me the blasphemy, then."

"We will not take God's name in vain - yet we will ask questions that may put it into people's minds that - that God will have another child, got on another virgin."

As she spoke, she knew her suit was hopeless. Newbury, so careful on God's behalf, would never countenance this.

"Will you pray with me?" asked Newbury, "While I try to find God's will?"

"Gladly," said Cat, surprised to have this small chance.

She knelt, and closed her eyes, and could think of nothing further to ask, and so buried her own will in a fervent wish to be God's child, to serve His will, to not wake some day and find her life mis-spent.

She opened her eyes at last, to find Newbury's eyes steady on her.

"Have you prayed?" Cat asked.

"You are so sure," Newbury said, "that God is not offended by what you do, what Bruno does."

Cat sighed. "Yes - altogether sure."

"Suppose you taught this art of yours to Parker."

"I don't think he would learn it from me."

"Suppose he learned it of another."

"Well, then, suppose he did?"

"Parker still believes that you are an animal. Suppose he came to you and asked you if you would be his familiar?"

"He should not - he feels badly towards me. And I am not enough different from him. And I would not agree to it."

"Suppose he would have it so. And suppose he saw you different enough. And suppose that when you denied him your agreement, he nodded as though he heard the bleating of a sheep, and went his way, and did what he would. Would it truly hurt you in no way to be so used by him?"

Cat felt tears start to her eyes. "If I knew of it - it would make me uneasy. If I knew -"

"And do you not believe that God knows all things?" asked Newbury, gently.

Cat had seen the trap, an instant before it was sprung. And it had her truly - for she had used many animals as familiars, and sometimes the words she spoke, to ask their favour, had been in her head alone, and the animal some way off. Her long years in Somerset's house would have been unbearable without the freedom of her mind.

Suppose Parker had asked her favour in the privacy of his mind, and believed it truly granted - and not so important, anyway, merely a formality to free his mind, not truly of concern to her, she being only a dull animal?

Cat bowed herself, and rocked, looking for some way out of this twist in her mind.

"There," said Newbury, "that will do. I know you love God, and I have made your head hurt a little, for all the times my head has hurt because of you. God alone knows why I needed both, but I did. Now - what must I do to help Elizabeth, and her child?"

Cat looked up, and saw Newbury grinning as merrily as she ever had. She dismissed her own bewilderment until later, and stepped forward uncertainly. Newbury caught her into an embrace that near smothered her, then set her back.

"Speak, will you? If I will not have you roasted by Elizabeth, no more will I have her torn open by a mob, and her babe die so. Did you truly think it of me?"

"If it was God's will -"

"I believe in no such God. He clothed us in flesh, and gave us a world to cherish, not to scorn and belittle. Those who savage the flesh to free the soul - they are a poor audience, breaking the company's properties and pinching the actors when they should be hearing the words the actors speak. I have always tried to be God's best audience - to hear every word, and praise every sunset. Now - speak!"

"You must - you must continue as you are. That is all. Court her favour on behalf of your brothers, while her belly grows large. Ask no questions, and answer none, but make it seem by your own certainty that no questions need to be answered."

"So - I will be her rock. And yours, too. That I can do, and if she send for my brothers soon, they will help her the more. They know my love for her, and they have loved me their whole life. Now go and weave your web a little stronger - I have seen the abyss it holds us from."

Cat nodded, but held her place.

"First - there is a thing I must do. Will you hear me do it, and help me?"

"I will hear you."

"Suppose. Suppose Elizabeth is too frightened to go to Bruno, because he sees much, and will not keep secrets. Suppose she will not come to me, because - because she believes I thought her faithless. Though that is never what I did think! Suppose she seeks comfort, and my Dudley's shoulder begins to look broad and comfortable as a good bed."

Cat looked at Newbury's puzzled frown.

"That should do it - Bruno is a very clever idiot, and I am a very wise fool. And my mother knows everything. Now - let's go."

Cat reached Bruno's door, and thumped the heel of her hand on the door. The stick was not across the window, so he worked, but could be disturbed.

He opened the door with no word of greeting, and with a blankness of expression she was unoffended by.

Cat and Newbury slipped inside, found a place for themselves, and watched as he paced, muttering. Cat began to think they should leave and come again, but Newbury held her wrist and wouldn't let her slip away.

"Cat is afraid that Elizabeth still loves Dudley," she said.

"Newbury!"

Bruno looked from one to another, seeming to come back from a long way distant.

"Is that so great a problem?" he asked finally.

Cat bit her lip. "I love Elizabeth. I love Dudley. The thought of him loving her as he loves me makes me wish to rip each shred of hair from her head, and throw him into a pond. I think it is ugly of me, and I cannot change it."

Bruno smiled a little - then laughed enormously. Cat knew why he laughed, but kept a carefully blank face, trying to look, if anything, a little offended.

"Do you think I can help you with this?" he asked.

"Clearly you are turning over some great problem," she said, "Clearly -"

"It is done," he said, "It is complete. What you saw were the last of the birthing pains. I have now, within my memory palace, a set of ledgers which will allow me for all time to leave alone any place that any man believes is proper to God alone. The secret was in scripture, oddly enough. Did you know that the Hebrews wrote down only the hard sounds of their language? The rest is really a keeping of space, and they gave, moreover, a number to each letter that corresponded to a hard sound. I know not the exact correspondence, yet I have formulated a math, with base of ten, for that I know the importance of fives and tens, whereby any word may be represented by a number, and any number by a word."

"Oh," said Cat.

"Take, for example, your own name, sweet Cat - that would be represented by seven and one, or seventy-one. Newbury is harder - that would be... two hundred and ninety four!"

"And the point of this?" asked Newbury. "Would you wish to multiply me by Cat?"

Bruno laughed again, "A pretty notion! Yes, pretty indeed, I will think on it later."

Cat resolved to herself never to ask Bruno what happened when Cat was multiplied by Newbury. In some ways, it was more dangerous to deal with a man addicted to honesty, than with one accustomed to deceit.

"But, no - the point of it is only this. I can compose ledgers in my mind, as large as need be, in which the first thing stored is held by a thing representing one. One is to be represented by the sound 'd', since I have observed many times that it is the first hard sound a baby tries, and I believe it significant. 't' is analogous to 'd', in its formation within the mouth, so that that also means one. Now I require a word with an association of singularity. I have dismissed 'toe' which carries an association with 'ten', although it is itself singular. I am torn between 'hat' and 'hut'."

"So much thinking!" cried Newbury, "And you have not even 'one' yet?"

"Ah, but 'one' is hard - both zero and two are easier. Zero is 'ice' - for I can think of nothing more like nothing - if you see what I mean - than a landscape that is all ice. When the sky is flat white," he said dreamily, "and you reach a place where the ice is perfect - it is like being suspended in nothing."

"You have visited such a place?" asked Cat, wonderingly.

"Only in my mind," Bruno said dismissively. "'Two', now - is 'Noah'. It is the only possibility. And think - I have already both seventy-one, and seventy-two."

With that, he blushed, and Cat laughed, suddenly knowing, if she was 'seventy-one', exactly who would be 'seventy-two', her very sister number, and knowing, therefore, exactly why Bruno blushed.

"Something is funny?" asked Bruno.

"There is another possibility for two," said Cat easily. "Could not the word 'one' represent 'two', as readily as the word 'Noah'? And then 'two' could represent 'one'."

Bruno looked horrified. "No!" he said. "That is not funny."

Cat did her best to look repentant, rather than relieved, and Bruno gathered himself to continue.

"Three is represented by 'womb' - this being at once a tripartite organ - have you ever seen a sheep dissected? No. And then it is also the means by which two becomes, in worldly terms, three. Four is 'arrow' - there being four directions only that an arrow may fly in."

"Hundreds, surely?" asked Newbury.

"In a way, hundreds yet they are all ad-mixtures of only four cardinal directions." Cat frowned, thinking of an arrow shot straight into the air but said nothing.

"Five is aisle as when you were married, Cat, do you remember? You, and a maid to stand with you. Your husband, and a man to stand with him. Me, to marry you. Hence, five."

"I see," said Cat, gravely, although she thought this was his weakest piece of reasoning so far.

"Six is shoe. Look, I'll show you," and Bruno ripped off his right shoe, placed his foot beside it, and counted, five toes on his foot, followed by the great toe that was his shoe. Cat caught Newbury eye, and both laughed.

"Seven is cow. There is a riddle I have come across in most of the countries I have passed through. In its most simple version, it is stated thus: four stiff standers, two sharp pointers, and a dangle. Seven, do you see? Eight watch this," he said, and held up his fingers, four on each hand, and interlinked them, so that four seemed warp, and four weft. Cat had never seen fingers bend as much as Bruno's did to achieve this feat, and she was relieved when he released them from the tangle.

"Eight is weave. Nine is bee - bee being analogous to a cow, except in having six legs, two seeking devices, and one sting. There is much of my creation still to work out yet I think it promising that I have already milk, and honey. Ten is another that is ridiculously easy see!" and he tore off his other shoe, waggling all of his toes at them, "Toes!"

Cat and Newbury clung helplessly together, so taken by mirth that they could not speak.

Finally, Newbury gasped, "So much work, so much thought, in order that you will avoid intruding into God's thoughts. You must truly love Him."

Cat looked, horrified, from Bruno to Newbury, feeling the abyss open again under her.

"Parthenian!" she said, it being the only word in the front of her mind, to forestall Bruno's fatal honesty.

"Parthenian?" he asked, genuinely puzzled.

"Parthenian birth", she said, "One become two. Used mainly of Mary but also of Adam. And I have heard it spoken of as science, rather than theology."

"Yes!" he exclaimed. "Those small animalcules, seen in unclean water, which are first one, then paff! two smaller, exactly like the parent. Still, he said, in the context of the work I do here, using one to give two is is confusion entire."

"Think you," Cat asked, "That something larger than an animalcule could ever give birth so? To one exactly like itself? If, as is believed, my daughters and sons are nested whole within me, and daughters and sons already in the daughters within me - could not some means be found to wake just one of my daughters?"

Bruno frowned. "Why would you wish it?" he asked. "Have you not a husband?"

"Yes, of course," said Cat, "In fact, that is why I asked. My husband laments that our children will owe something to him, as well as me. This grieves me not even slightly, of course - but he would have one, just one daughter, who is as like me as may be, since he never saw me as a child." Cat, twining two fingers together behind her back, resolved to make this wish known to Dudley as soon as she saw him next, confident that it would enchant him convincingly.

Bruno frowned. "Dee might know," he said musingly. "It is not something that I am vastly curious about... Two from one," he said, his eyes growing satisfyingly vague, "One become two."

Cat began to steal away, feeling her work well done - Newbury held her with a gesture, though, and she paused. Newbury stole forward, darting laughing glances first at Cat, then at the rapt Bruno. At last, she pulled his shoes from under his very nose, still without exciting his attention, and, hugging them to her chest, strolled past Cat to wait at the door. Cat opened the door, and Newbury fled past her.

"What are you doing?" Cat asked.

"Trying something. I've always wondered how truly distant he was when that look came on him. Now I know. And, oh, Cat, I've had no fun since you were gone. And Bruno's solution - it will work for you too! I am so glad."

"Bruno's solution?" Cat had forgotten she had a pressing worry still in need of a solution.

"His new art! I saw you, making jokes in his new language, as if it had always been yours. It is God-given, being able to do in moments what would take me months, and believe I would find no merriment in it. This is the path God intends for your wits, I am sure of it."

Cat could find no answer.

Newbury looked at her sidelong. "I wager you remember every number he told you - nothing to ten. Try!"

Cat shrugged. "If I do remember, it is his credit for being so vivid. Nothing is ice. One is - hut. It is a more solid 'one' than 'hat'," and besides, she thought, a hat goes on top of ones head, and that will lead me into old paths too readily, "and will hold more treasure. Two is Noah. Although some animals, you know, went in by fourteens. Still. Three is womb. Four, arrow. Five, aisle. Six," she chuckled gently, and prodded one of the shoes Newbury carried, "Shoe. Seven, cow. Eight, weave. Nine, bee. Ten toes, and there we have it. Excepting seventy-one, which is Cat, and seventy-two, which is Queen. And two hundred and ninety-four, which is Newbury. Does it not trouble you that he uses you as one of his numbers?" Cat asked, curious at the turning of Newbury's mind.

"No! It is like - he uses a picture of me, or writes my name into a book. To write a name is certainly not sin, be it God's name, or mine. It has not the - sulphurous reek that your talk of familiars carried."

Cat nodded, seeing the distinction as Newbury saw it. She wondered if this new art would work in place of the one she had owned since she was first looking at the world. Looking at Newbury, glowing so with delight, she decided she could make it work.

Cat returned to her rooms well content with her afternoon's work, full to the brim of well-earned pride in her clever tongue. She rejoiced to find Dudley there - so much better to tie the one loose end in her discourse, and know that all was made as safe as she could make it.

"Where have you been?" he asked, in tones she could not recognise as his.

"Newbury and I have been to see Giordano," she said, hearing something in her own voice that she did not like to find there.

"I thought you and Newbury could no longer be friends," he said suspiciously - it wasn't quite a question. "I understood that I was to accompany you always to see the Signor. 'Giordano', you call him now? That is new."

Tears pricked, unbidden, at Cat's eyes.

"What is this?" she asked.

He stood. "There is a puzzle doing the rounds, it seems. It has been long in circulation - but people's kindness has kept it from my ears until now. Do you know the puzzle already?"

"I know it not. Yet I am good at puzzles - ask it of me."

"It goes this way. If ladies go always in twos, to visit a solitary priest, how be it that a serving-man might hear - might hear noises betokening affection from an inner room, when neither - when neither - " His voice, it seemed, grew too hoarse to continue.

"Damn you, girl," he said after a moment, "Why look you so frightened? Is it not only a puzzle?"

Cat's mind raced. "Do people put a name to either lady?" she asked.

"They need not. The answer to the puzzle is - 'African practices'. The palace is not, you will note, greatly burdened with Africans at this time, nor has it been for many months."

Cat winced at the burden of sarcasm in his voice.

"You do not rush, I notice, to defend your reputation," he said dully.

"Nor will I," said Cat. "My life I promised, in return for favours unasked - I will not withold my reputation."

"Elizabeth?" he spat, "How could this touch Elizabeth?"

"She has visited Bruno," Cat said calmly, "In company with an African. More an African than I am - and more than once."

"Bruno - and your mother?" asked Dudley, aghast. "She is comely enough - I grant you, she does not look her age. She -"

"She is not the issue here," said Cat.

"No," said Dudley, "I will not believe such things of Elizabeth. None would."

"If," Cat ventured delicately, "If it were not a matter of," her face showed her distaste with the words, "'African practices'. If it were a matter of great passion, and a blind eye turned? Then could you believe?"

"Not easily," he said, sounding more like her Dudley.

"If her belly began to grow great, in a very short time from now," she asked. "Then could you?"

"Oh, my God," he said, more in tones of prayer, than of casual blasphemy.

"The sad thing is," she said, "That not only my reputation is needed, to give the puzzle the answer it must have, and that right soon. If the tale called for a man happily cuckolded, the part could be played by you, and I believe you would play it with a will. But that is not what is asked for. I told Newbury her part in saving Elizabeth would be simple, and easy. I did not know I lied."

She turned, to leave the room - then at the last moment, paused to tie one knot in her precarious tapestry.

"If any ask," she said, "You wish for a daughter. One that is very like to me."

"But with hair of crimson, not amber hue?" asked Dudley mockingly, and Cat flinched, unable to tell if he mocked himself, or her, or the world at large

Cat felt weary, as if she could not move a step. All her lightness, all her pleasure, had drained from her, and so much work still to do. Yet she could not leave this now that she knew of it - she had no way of knowing whether any suspicion yet turned on Elizabeth. She must act as soon as may be.

She found her way to Newbury's rooms, and tapped gently on the door.

Newbury opened them, and Cat watched her first joy fade into a reflection of her own troubled aspect. She pulled Cat into the room, and shut the door swiftly.

"What has happened?" she asked, "Oh! Is Elizabeth well? Does the babe trouble her? Is the babe... ?"

Cat shook her head, "As well as I know, they both go safely. But I am foresworn. I told you your part in this would be simple and easy - it will not be so. Not if you truly wish to save Elizabeth, and her babe."

"Tell me?"

"There is a puzzle, among the worldly in the palace. How is it - if ladies go always two together to see a certain priest - that sounds of affection might be heard, coming from an inner room. It is an ugly thing."

Newbury considered this for a moment. "Could it not be any of the ladies who go to be amused by Bruno? There are many."

"The answer to the riddle is 'African practices'."

Newbury's lips parted. "African practices? What are they?"

Cat scowled, "I know no more than you do. Same as 'Italian practices', I should think, or 'French practices' - an excuse to gloat over things that are no one's business but God's and two people's."

Newbury bit her lip, and bowed her head in mute apology.

Cat's scowl faded. "Newbury, I am sorry - I am not angry with you. It is you should be angry - for there are only two women in the palace who have visited Bruno in company with an African, and one of them is Elizabeth. People - I think people want us to be the two. It is safer, certainly, and we are both young and still toothsome. But I don't know that it's fixed altogether, yet, and it must be, well before Elizabeth's appearance calls attention to her. Will you help?"

Newbury stooped to pick something from the floor.

"Well - I know now why I took these," she said, holding out Bruno's two shoes.

"You will help then? It is the end of your hopes of marriage."

"My hopes of marriage. No more keeping my blessed hands white," she said, looking down at them, around the rough brown shoes.

She looked up, and caught Cat's pitying look.

"You think me brave," she said, and laughed with a convincing merriness.

"I think you must be," said Cat.

Newbury grew sober again. "You wish to act soon, I can see that. And I do see what part I am to play. But we have a little time - the man who takes meats to Bruno comes first to the Dame in the next room to mine, and she always wants to talk to him, and talks very loud to penetrate her own ears. When we hear them, that is the time to seek out Bruno. Until then, there is a story I think you should hear."

"Tell me," said Cat.

"Once upon a time," said Newbury, "there was a young girl who had an unsuitable friend. His name was William, sweet William with the wide brow and great ambitions. He was quite of the wrong station, so this girl sneaked to see him, although in truth all they ever did was talk, swap songs and stories."

Newbury was quiet a moment, and Cat, who thought she saw where the story tended, began rehearsing ways to suggest that, while it might seem first love must be last love, it was not always so.

"William travelled with a group of players. The girl badgered her parents incessantly to take her to the last night of their play - and planned to meet William the next morning, to say goodbye. The part he played that night was - was a young maid, tender-hearted, but with all William's ready wit. I realised that William could only be my friend - yet the maid he might have been, might have been far more."

Newbury looked full into Cat's uncomprehending eyes. "I stayed in my rooms the next day, pleading fatigue. I wanted to see William, to say goodbye, yet I had no words to explain what I had felt the night before. To say nothing seemed dishonest - yet it seemed that anything I did say must be misconstrued, must damage our friendship much more than mere parting would.

"Since then, I have been - torn. It seemed I must some day marry. It seemed I would be foresworn even as I gave my vows, knowing I could be no true and honest wife. I thought of finding refuge in a convent. I might have done so, had I loved God less. But there were two things. Thing the first: I did not think celibacy was what God wanted of me my whole life. Thing the second: for as long as celibacy was seemly, it would be easier in court than among great numbers of women who were bright of mind, and pure of heart. I would not spend my life as a fox in a hen-run, trying to be pious and meek, and failing betimes.

"There you have it. While many women in the palace think you lucky in your marriage - I see only Dudley's luck."

Cat was saved from finding any reply by the closing of a door near by, and the raising of a voice. Newbury tucked both shoes under her arm, and offered a hand to Cat. Cat took it, and they sped together out of the palace, through the garden in gathering twilight. Cat looked around with new eyes, finding the world strange, enchanted. They arrived at Bruno's door, and Cat lifted the stick, placing it across the window so that no knock would disturb what was to happen.

In a way, it was absurdly easy. They had discussed nothing, rehearsed nothing - yet as Newbury handed the shoes to Bruno, Cat slipped through the door to his bedchamber. When he followed Cat, protesting, Newbury followed him, and placed her back firmly to the door, so that he must manhandle her to leave.

"There is a matter," Cat said, "of Cat multiplied by Newbury."

"My ladies - a poor jest. I meant nothing."

Cat looked down, and plucked at the ties to her bodice. When she looked up, Bruno had his cheek turned into the wall, his eyes closed. Her eyes flew to Newbury, and she saw pity there, as Newbury also unfastened her bodice. Hearing a sound in the outer room, Newbury opened the door and backed through, eyes always on Cat. Cat advanced on her - and met the astonished eyes of a serving-man with a platter of meats. Cat cried out, in a way that felt false, yet when Newbury turned, cried out, turned back and swept Cat with her into the inner chamber, her shock seemed real enough to carry all.

Cat wondered if Newbury felt as shamed as she did, looking at Bruno. She found in herself no willingness to mislead him, but said only, "I'm sorry - it was necessary." And she turned half away from him to fasten her bodice, though she kept her face toward him.

Bruno looked sharply into her face. "Necessary?"

"I truly believe so."

Bruno's gaze flew round the room. "Then I must leave. Should have left by now. I thank you for your service ladies." He would not look at them, but continued scanning the room as if trying to decide what he should take, what he should leave.

As soon as they were decent again, Cat and Newbury passed through the garden, twined arm in arm.

Newbury would have gone her way from Cat inside the great door, but Cat held fast to her.

"Come to my rooms," she said, "please?"

Newbury looked at her curiously, but followed her, asking no questions.

"So - is it done? Are my horns quite firmly fixed?" asked Dudley as the door opened, not turning to look.

"In the eyes of the world, yes. Not in the eyes of God," said Cat, wondering how she could call back her Dudley.

"What - Bruno did not find you tempting? I am insulted. Perhaps I should call him out."

"You should hurry, then. He will be leaving as soon as may be."

Now Dudley turned, and Cat felt some pity at the pain evident behind his anger.

"Newbury!" said Dudley. "Well met. Am I also to see your little show? Mayhap I will be a less disappointing audience than Bruno was."

"Oh, I find you disappointing enough," said Newbury coolly.

Dudley flushed, and advanced on Newbury.

She continued speaking, in level tones. "I find I have little sympathy with you. I might feel more, did I know exactly what you suffer, but I fear it is a book forever closed to me. I will never know what it is," she paused momentarily, "What it is to share a marriage that seems ordained by God. I will never know the envy of the worldly, at my possession of a rare and precious creature. I will never know what it is to lose the outward show of such a marriage, and keep only the substance of it. As I said: I will never know your pain."

For the first time, Dudley's mask broke. "Newbury - God, Newbury, forgive me."

Newbury did not answer immediately, but first disentangled her arm from Cat's.

"It has been - a long day. I find myself weary. Cat - if you would forgive your husband on my behalf, I would count it a most gentle service."

After Newbury left, Dudley knelt before Cat, all penitence. "Can you? Forgive me?"

"It seems I must," said Cat, then softened, "And it will be no great hardship." She stooped to embrace him, flooded with gratitude.

Later, he spoke against her hair. "You must think me faithless. Yet - I have felt you cooling towards me. If you deny it, I'll call myself mistaken, and never ask again. Yet - you have cooled."

Cat turned within his embrace. "I am more careful, I'll allow. We have been many months married. I think we may be no longer alone in our marriage bed - but I wanted to be past the first weeks before I spoke. Many times, the first weeks are also the last weeks. I was almost ready to speak to you - and you are the first I've told, although my mother may have known before I did. She has a more than wise eye. You may have that daughter - although, all considered, you might find you prefer a son - or - "

"Or?" Dudley pressed.

"The timing is bad," she said gently. "People will count, and wait, and look hard at any child that comes soon to us. If - "

"People can look all they may, and see what they will," said Dudley firmly. "I will openly covet a daughter, and quietly welcome a son, if it be a son you carry. And Newbury should stand godmother to any child we have, for she made me see, clearer than I ever hoped to see again, what a great blessing it is to have held you in my arms even once, to hope to do so even once more. A child - I pray you are right, and I pray it goes well with the child, and if you wish to banish me from your bed, I will go this instant."

Cat gripped him firmly around his waist, feeling delicious sleep almost in her reach. "You must stay," she said, "Loneliness would not be good for me at this time. I must have comfort."

"Then comfort you shall have," said Dudley, and they shifted against each other into their accustomed positions for sleep.

Bruno was the last to petition Elizabeth the next day. Her warmth towards him was apparent, but cooled as he presented his request.

"Has my service grown wearisome to you, then?" she asked, coldly now.

"No. I wish to continue in your service, my whole life if you will have it. And if you will not have my service, I will yet remain in your kingdom, and be always your loyal subject. Yet your kingdom is large. I would know its farther reaches, and return to speak of them. I have devised a new art of memory - it chivvies my heels, and demands food. I have greatly enjoyed my time in your court - and I am sure there is more to be learned here. God willing, and your Highness granting, I will return to learn it, and to speak of what I have learned elsewhere."

Elizabeth frowned. "And if I would have you remain here?"

Bruno sighed. "Highness, you have often told me that to have the loyalty of your subjects, you must know their concerns."

"That is true. Do I not listen carefully when my subjects speak of their concerns to me?"

"You do. And it makes you a good queen. To be a great queen, however, you must know the concerns of those who do not seek you out, who remain far from court. Those who fear to speak: those who wish only to build a life with their own means. They are no less your people than those who seek you out, and if you are to build a strong nation, they will be its foundation."

Elizabeth closed her eyes briefly, then said, "This art you speak of - you have not yet begun to teach it to me. I would have that be part of your service to me."

Bruno frowned. "Your Highness' interest is most gracious and flattering. I have prepared documents, setting out the principles of the new art. I would be honoured to leave them safe in your hands. However, I know the pressures of your court - I could not presume to occupy an adequate space of time to begin an honest teaching."

Elizabeth looked down at her linked hands. Cat, having watched the whole exchange, admired her calm. Her mother touched her arm to request her attention.

"Bring Newbury to me, would you? I have aught to ask her."

Cat nodded, and made her way swiftly, straight across the floor. Newbury twined arms with her, and they returned the same way.

"Be then my best ambassador, an ambassador to my own people," said Elizabeth, as Cat and Newbury passed, and Bruno bowed, and turned, solemn, from the throne. He almost collided with Newbury, flushed crimson, and hurried away with stammered apologies, all his gathered dignity lost.

Cat and Newbury arrived before Cat's mother.

"You wished to speak with me?" asked Newbury.

"Did I?" she asked, "Lord, it grows harder and harder for me to keep one thing in my head. Never mind, child." And she turned, and left the audience chamber. Cat looked after her, suspicious.

A few days later, Bruno being well gone, and near forgotten in the swift-moving currents of court, Cat followed her mother's instructions, and began dressing to exaggerate her pregnancy, rather than to diminish it. Dudley, as promised, was vocal in wishing for a daughter, as like to Cat as might be possible. Dee sought him out, and offered several suggestions, most of which seemed likely to prove injurious to either Cat's or their child's life. Dudley placed his faith in God's provenance, and Dee lost interest in Cat, which was some relief to her. She could not like the way his eyes rested on her, and she well remembered that while Dee had sought out Bruno, Bruno had privately dismissed Dee. "Muddles and mess," he had concluded, and that was that.

The months following flew by. All decisions being made, Elizabeth gave herself over to serenity, turning aside all questions with a simple, "God's will be done," turning more and more to her advisers to continue work she had begun. The only project she increased her work on, it being gentle exercise for the mind alone, was her study of Bruno's new art. Cat worked at it as diligently as she, and even Newbury began her first steps in any of the arts of memory, wishing to encourage converts to this new art, and away from the two arts that she felt were dangerous to a practitioner's soul.

As Elizabeth's condition grew more apparent, Dee and the court physician both haunted her, the physician suspecting a malady that had afflicted her half-sister, Mary, both wishing to examine her. Elizabeth declared herself safe in God's hands, and kept her body to herself. Cat's mother examined Cat, but Elizabeth then would only ask questions, and listen gravely to the answers.

Cat and Elizabeth went often to the chapel together, Newbury sometimes joining them. They prayed quietly, and also for show, and started quite a fashion for piety.

During this time, there came a ship from a new land - a land offering much gold, in addition to new plants and animals.

Cat watched with pride as Elizabeth quietly explained to the ship's captain just what the difference was between spreadable things, and shareable things, and also the difference between what was real, and what was agreed.

"These," she said, holding in her hands the strange, bulbous roots he had given her, coloured like parsnips, but shaped like stones smoothed by a stream, "These are spreadable - they will grow here in the land they are given, and they will grow just as much in the land they came from, not one whit diminished. Gold is shareable - each tiny bit of gold taken across the sea, diminishes the gold left, and the more that is taken, the more it will be diminished.

"Moreover," she went on, "These are real - the more we grow them, the more value they will have - the more mouths filled with savour, the more stomachs with nourishment, the more bodies made strong and straight. The value of gold is an agreed value only. If you bring more gold here, the value of this pretty thing around my neck will decrease, little by little. Would you will that, Captain?"

He frowned, and shook his head, but slowly, puzzled, without conviction.

Elizabeth reached up, and unfastened the pendant around her neck - a single pearl, set in gold.

"Wear this," she said. "Think of what I have said - try the ideas in your own mind, test them as you will. Remember what I ask - that this be the only gold to cross the ocean with you, and that it always return alone, with you. We will seek what is real, and spreadable, and good, and we will return like for like. Gold is a place-marker, between people who will meet again many times. It is a convenience among such people - it has no place between people who may meet only once."

The captain frowned. "It may be that I will come to agree with your ideas, having given them thought, as you say. Yet there are others on my ship besides me - and most of them are on the ship for gold, or glory, or both. I don't see that changing because I stand up in front of them and say you would have it so."

Elizabeth looked down again at the roots that lay in her hand. "I have heard it said that a fair exchange is no robbery. It follows then, does it not, that anything - anything! - short of a fair exchange is robbery. There may be gold in robbery - that being the point. Yet, surely, there can be no glory?"

"Highness - if I travelled with monks, they might see it so. It is not monks I travel with."

Parker edged closer to the conversation, listening intently. Cat redoubled her own attention, seeing the light that took Elizabeth's face at the mention of monks. Soon, Cat thought, soon there would be monks on board ship, partly for the show of piety - partly for piety's own sake. Elizabeth was kind to those few remnants of the old religion that escaped her father's persecution, and Parker half-encouraged her, while standing ready to resist any strong advantage given outside his remit. So it began to be that two together, one of the old religion, one of the new, were most like to succeed in any petition offered, and a few such partnerships had begun.

Elizabeth sighed. "Captain - it is true, what you say. It is not possible to herd people onto God's path. Yet - if a strong example be set before them, from one they are already disposed to admire?"

Cat herself admired the light that shone in Elizabeth's eyes as she beheld the captain. The captain himself seemed to grow a little in stature. Elizabeth continued. "What would you, you yourself, see as fair exchange for this foodstuff I hold here? Apples, perhaps?"

The captain shook his head. "They'd not survive the journey - when we arrived, they'd be rotted, every one."

"Well - they could still be planted, could they not? You could be careful to take those whose children would be true to the parent. You could take rootstock also, could you not?"

"Highness - it would be years before a single apple was plucked from a tree, rootstock or no."

"And then, if we returned after years, they would know us to be honest and benevolent - not so?"

The captain shook his head once more. "My men want gold and glory. Virtue is a slow-growing plant that they'll none of, I tell you."

Elizabeth stepped forward. "Bring me three men - three who will as you say they will. Three who fear not to speak, as well as listen. Let me be an example before them, and try what will happen."

"These be not gentle folk, Highness. If they offend you -"

"If they offend me, the blame is theirs and mine, and none of yours. Let me try this."

Days later, came three men to Elizabeth, suspiciously well-scrubbed for men of their station. A few of the court, Parker among them, stood close enough to hear what was said, but did not seek to join the conversation.

As Elizabeth spoke, two nodded gratifyingly, but the third, the youngest, shook his head.

Elizabeth turned her attention full on him.

"You do not see that true glory -"

"I care nothing for glory. I want gold, and that right fast."

Elizabeth frowned, and backed away half a step, unthinking. One of the man's companions nudged him roughly, but he shouldered him aside and stood his ground as Elizabeth stepped forward and spoke again.

"Gold is but an agreed thing - it cannot be eaten or drunk, it will not protect you from the cold. It is pretty, surely, but so is a daisy, think you not?"

"Gold will buy me back to my mother's farm. Daisies will do no such."

"If your mother's farm is where you would be, I wonder why you left it?"

"Aye, I wonder that, too. I woke with a swollen head, and coin in my pocket, and the word of the ship-master that I'd taken the coin willing. And the floor moving under me, as it never moved in all the other times I'd taken too much of ale in the village."

Elizabeth frowned. "Behind your wish for gold, is a wish for freedom. Your tale is the tale of a man tricked into slavery. If it is gold that is needed to buy you free, that is gold that I might pay, and pay gladly, if you are the only such in my navy. Are you?"

The man shook his head. "Four others on our ship, that I know of. One has nothing to buy himself free for any more. I'd not be like him. The others of us are laying coin aside - the price out is always higher than the price in."

"That is one ship spoken for. I miss Bruno - he would have seen at once, all the questions to be asked, and had answers for half of them before I'd begun speaking. Still - I can see the next thing to do, and see it done, too. Tell me a thing. I would be just to all my subjects, and yet I am one woman, and cannot speak to all of them. What I can do, is pick one, and let him speak for all that are like him in a certain way - one washerwoman for all washerwomen, so to speak, one pressed sailor for all like him. It is a heavy burden to ask someone to take. Will you take it?"

The man straightened and frowned, as if trying his shoulders against a load. He nodded. "I'll speak as I find."

"How long have you been trying to free yourself?"

"Two voyages. About three years. I thought I had the thing done, once, but before the voyage end, I'd been fined half my store of coin for speaking out of turn. I offered them to take it from my flesh, but they'd not. Not that time."

"Do you think - are you as good a sailor as you would be if you were willing?"

"I'm not the worst. It's not in me to hold back on what's set me to do - and yet, I've seen men who do what's set, and go find more to do. That's not me - I'll be off dreaming of home when my work's done."

"Will you pray to find a way free and home, doing no hurt to those who've held you unwilling?"

He looked down at his hands. "Sometimes that's all I want. Sometimes - it's true, and I'll say it - there's an anger in me that would have bloody vengeance. I think - most times, even when the black mood is heavy on me, if what I wanted were set before me, I'd turn aside from it. I'd take my freedom, and leave revenge."

"That is God's path. There are many roads into slavery, and only three out. The first, that failed in Exodus for want of Pharaoh's understanding, is side by side, slave-keeper and slave finding their way to freedom together, for I know in my heart one cannot keep slaves and be free. The second is the way described in Leviticus - renouncing the rewards of slavery that have been dreamed of for many years, retiring to a wilderness and spending a long time hungry, and with hungry children. That is a hard path, but still better than the third, which is the path taken by those that covet the rewards of slavery: the path of blood, of theft and vengeance. That is a hard path to turn back from, and as long as it is followed, it leads only to more blood, and away from freedom.

"One more question - I've said I have coin to buy you free. I have not coin to buy free all like you, not that and do all else that I must do. It may be you can see the answer I want - and yet you must give the answer you yourself want. You can be free now - you alone, of all like you - or you can wait and be free with the others. What would you?"

Parker, who stood close, interrupted then. "It is obvious where his best interest lies - there is no question, surely?"

The young sailor looked hard at Parker, and then back at Elizabeth, but continued to think.

Finally he said, "I'd stay, until all like me are free. My bunkmate and I, we watch each other's back. I'd not leave until he can go, too."

Elizabeth smiled, then Parker muttered, "Probably his catamite."

The sailor stepped forward. "What did he say?"

Elizabeth held one hand up. "It matters not what he said. He spoke of matters that may be true, or may be false, but which are not in any way relevant. Whether you are unwilling allies with your bunkmate, or true friends, or yet more - that is no one's affair but your own."

Parker spoke louder now. "If they sin, that is then my affair, surely?"

Elizabeth kept an even and gentle tone. "If they seek that of God within each other - if they care each for the other's well-being - if they do no harm to any third person - then there is no sin - I would stake my own soul on it. Great risk, always - but there is great risk also in going upon the ocean, and we treasure greatly those who do so with a willing heart." With that, her smile embraced the two sailors who before had accepted her words unquestioning, and they, who had begun to seem a little estranged, warmed within the circle of her approval.

"One thing more I'd ask of you - all of you. Will you pray for me, to find God's path in this matter? Even where God's path is a path not yet built?"

Two nodded. The third - contrary again - chewed his lip a little. "If it please you - I would like better to pray that you find God's path in all matters." He stepped back upon one heel, a little wary.

Elizabeth's smile struck him like the sun.

"It pleases me. And I will pray the same for you - if you wish it so?" Again, she included all three in the question - and this time, all three nodded.

The flying months gave way to dragging days. Cat found her easy stride impeded by her bulk, more to the left side than the right, and began to resent her mother's insistence on frequent walking around the garden.

"The world press down on you, your whole life. You can let it hurt you, or you can let it help you. Stay on your feet, world is your friend at this time. Lie on your back, world will torture you. Rest any way you like, but stay off your back, or you are nothing but stranded turtle, or dying sheep."

Cat demanded solace from Dudley, a little shocked at the way her world had come down to cravings, and searching after comfort. She found it in her to admire Elizabeth's self-sufficiency, but would not copy it.

One day at dinner, Cat looked up to see Elizabeth's face drawn with pain. She hastened to Elizabeth's side, and she, and her mother and Kempe, all helped Elizabeth away from the table, and into the quiet of her own bedchamber.

Kempe took charge of Elizabeth, but made no objection to the others' presence. Elizabeth paced the floor, occasionally stopping to grip the great post at the foot of her bed, and shake it - or rather, shake herself against it, for she swayed madly, silently, while it moved not at all.

Hours went by so, with no real conversation, while the world outside the window darkened, and faint birdsong began to be heard.

When the lamps and candles were lit, Cat's mother went round and extinguished half of them.

"Mother! The queen of England need not worry over a few candles more or less. Especially at this time."

"She may be queen, but the body she wears is an animal - like a horse, or a cat, near enough. Shine bright light on a cat at this time, she'll slow to nothing. Same if too many strangers near. We can see well enough, and she don't need to see anything."

Cat frowned, and remembered other births, where she had assisted her mother. They had mostly happened in half dark, and in solitude, and with great quiet.

"It's true," said Kempe. "I watched, one of many, as Elizabeth's mother fought to give her child birth. People say she was brave the day she died - they should have seen her the day Elizabeth was born, gawked at by any who could wangle their way in, handled and pushed at by three different doctors. I was there to comfort her, and I was the only one. The rest might have been at a horse race - I heard bets made. And loud exclamations of horror, and speculation on whether she'd live or no. This is kindlier."

Cat had never heard Kempe speak so much, and had never felt so much in sympathy with the woman.

Before she could choose words, or even decide between speech and silence, she was gripped by a great pain, throughout the left side of her belly and back. She had felt her body tightening before this, and had enjoyed the sensation, tapping her rigid belly, and wondering if her time was close. There was no wondering now, though.

"Of all times," she said, a little breathless as her body released itself from the pain. "Why now?" she asked.

"Because God wills it, I would think," said her mother.

"I can leave," said Cat to Elizabeth, who leaned, watching, against the great post at the foot of the bed.

"Better if you stay," said her mother, "if you will have it so?" she asked Elizabeth.

Elizabeth nodded, and from then on, they paced the same stretch of carpet, and tugged, Elizabeth at the bedpost nearer the door, Cat at the bedpost nearer the window. It was amusing, almost, to note how they slipped into synchrony, and away again, like two girls on adjoining swings.

Cat had begun late, but raced ahead of Elizabeth, so that they looked together into the perfect, smeared face of Cat's daughter, before Elizabeth swung away to continue her pacing, and Kempe and Cat's mother wiped the babe, bound her belly, and wrapped her in cloths, before laying her again in Cat's welcoming arms. Cat divided her attention between her daughter's wise, open eyes, and Elizabeth's growing fatigue, and then looked only at her daughter, as Elizabeth reached extremity, and was helped by Cat's mother and Kempe. Cat had felt no embarassment at her own struggles - but now, calmer, she could not look at what was happening to Elizabeth.

Instead, she told over her babe's fingers, and toes, all perfect miniatures, down to the slender crescents at each fingertip. The down on the child's head was drying to a crimson fuzz. She brushed her lips across it, and breathed the child's scent, knowing the truth of her mother's assertions, that she was as much animal as any cat with only one kit.

Her reverie was interrupted by a child's cry - and then by Elizabeth's bitter voice.

"God is not done jesting," she said. "I have a son. How many mothers in this very bed have prayed for such? And all my prayers have rested on a daughter, for I remember well what you said. A son will have only a few years."

She turned her face aside on the pillow, and wept silent tears, not willing to even look at her son.

"Child," said Cat's mother, "sometimes it happens that God gives you the answer to a puzzle, as he gives you the puzzle itself. Not always - but sometimes."

Elizabeth looked at her, too weary to speak.

"It was God's will that these children be born together. I suggested it, and you approved it, but it could not have happened without his will."

Elizabeth shook her head slightly, slowly.

"I see what you are saying. I cannot ask it. Cat offered me her own life once - and I know she has given her good name to protect mine. It would be a devilish thing for me to ask her firstborn child from her. I am no gnome from a storybook."

"Some families would give much, to see their child set upon a throne," said Cat's mother, musingly.

"Some families. Not this family - I know Cat's concerns, they are not worldly."

Cat turned her attention closer upon her child, remembering a girl with leaf-green eyes, and very worldly wishes. Which was truly more troubling to the spirit, she wondered briefly - to be thought sinful when attempting nobility, or to be thought noble after courting sin?

"You need not ask," said Cat. "I will ask for you. Mother?" She held out her child to her mother, took the unwanted son from Kempe, trying how it would be. It was no fair exchange - her heart followed the one, while her eyes admired the other's likeness to her own child.

She saw from the corner of her eye, as her own child was set in Elizabeth's arms. Elizabeth frowned a little, but gathered the babe close to her, and looked into her eyes.

"I could love this child," said Elizabeth. She looked, for the first time, at Cat.

Cat bit her lip, and wondered how much time Elizabeth would truly have to love any child but her infant nation. Her frown cleared, as she pictured herself and her mother and Kempe, two children on the grass between them, Elizabeth away in the distance.

She looked harder at the child in her own arms. He drowsed, and she saw his eyes wander behind his half-closed lashes. She lifted him a little, and laid her cheek to his.

"I could love this child," she said.

"Then there is just Dudley to ask," said her mother.

"Dudley?" she asked, thinking, Dudley knows neither child - how can he miss what he has not known?

"People will look at the girl, and they will see Elizabeth. So much is clear already, yes?" she asked, and Kempe nodded her agreement.

"I saw Elizabeth when she was exactly this old - this could be that same infant."

Cat's mother nodded. "That is well. Who will they see when they look at the boy? Given who his mother is, and who his father?"

"Oh."

"Wait here," she said, and left them together on the great bed, shifting so close that the two babe's heads near touched. The girl's head began to turn aside, and Kempe showed Elizabeth how to help her search to fruition. Cat felt tears start to her eyes, and hoped Elizabeth would not see, and know why.

"I am fatigued," she told herself, and was pleased that the child in her own arms would rather sleep than hunger. Until the decision was completely made, she could not make the final leap into mothering him.

Dudley had been awake, waiting for Cat, and news of Elizabeth. He came straight away, and grasped the problem, and the proposed solution, swiftly. Yet he pondered before giving an answer.

"Are you happy for this child to inherit your lands?" asked Cat's mother.

"The greater bulk of the lands now mine, were given me by Elizabeth. I will not grudge them to her child. He will have dominion over any other son I might have - but then, so he should, in God's eyes, and it seems God's jest that my own daughter will have dominion over him.

"But the question you first asked me - it was not about my lands, but about my love. Can I love this child?"

Cat watched, torn, wishing above all for a swift end to the matter, so that she could begin gentling her spirit to whatever difficulties were ahead.

"It is like this," said Dudley slowly, "I know I should - and I believe I can. If Newbury be nearby to keep me honest. Otherwise - I will be cold, and hate myself for it, and that will make me colder. At some point, Cat will weary of it - and there will be no joy for any under our roof. I wish I were a better man, but I have wished as much in the past, and wishing has not yet made it so."

Cat's mother nodded, almost approvingly, and went to bring Newbury. She was slow to attend, having been asleep for some hours, and wishing at least to wash herself, and brush her hair, although she came in gown and bare feet, with hair loose. She heard the whole tale, and scowled fiercely at Dudley.

"I am the one hung horns upon your head - why would you want to keep me near?"

"You were also the one who showed me the horns were false. Cat brought you to our rooms because she feared to be alone with me - no," he said, shaking his head at Cat's protest, "If you were not afraid, you should have been. Newbury brought me back to my right senses, and I trust she will wake my love for this child, as surely as she reawakened my love for you."

Newbury's scowl was undiminished. "Nothing would please me more than to have a part in the raising of these children," she said, "but there is aught you should know. I swore, many years ago, that where I could, and where I must, I would be honest. Here, I must. If - if it is ever in my power to hang real horns upon your head, I will do it. Do you remember, Cat? I will not be a fox, trying to sleep in a henhouse. Every day, I would wake hungry, and one day I would be weak."

Dudley's mouth hung open with surprise. "You knew this?" he asked, turning on Cat.

She sought words. "She - she did not speak of any particular attraction towards me," she said finally.

"And if she had?" he asked. "What would you have felt?"

Cat closed her eyes, and wished that she could have back the night, and spend it sleeping with her child still in her, and Dudley still her loyal protector.

"In this matter," said Dudley, "I think long silence is answer enough. God is never done jesting is he?"

Elizabeth started, hearing her own words from Dudley's mouth.

"And yet sometimes, his jests are both gentle, and merry."

Cat opened her eyes, and stared at Dudley, wondering if it was truly his voice she had just heard.

"Here is the thing," he said, his voice remarkably matter-of-fact. "The thought of Bruno's eyes on you - not even his hands, but just his eyes - was unbearable to me. It was balm to my spirit when you told me that he averted his gaze. And it was further soothing to me when he sought me out, scant hours before he left us, and told me a thing you said. That as much as you loved Elizabeth, the thought of me loving her in the way that I loved you, made you want to snatch every hair from her head, and throw me into a pond. Was that true?"

Cat's face burned. "I said also that it was a thing I was not proud of."

Dudley smiled. "I should not have doubted either Bruno's memory, or his honesty. Thank you," he said, and bowed, most courtly. He turned to Newbury.

"You could have done great hurt to me, months ago, when you came to our rooms. Instead, you gave me back my marriage."

Newbury shook herself impatiently, as if to shed his generosity. "Cat's happiness rests on you - I have always known it. It is even more true now, when there are two children whose happiness rests on hers."

"Then you will safeguard their happiness, and Cat's, and mine will follow of its own. I fear you will find this belittling," he said. "When I think of your eyes on my wife, or your hands on my wife, I cannot mind it. And if I think of her eyes, or her hands, on you, it is as if she told me that she had conceived a passion for watercolour painting, or - or for Bruno's quaint numerology. It evokes no horror, no anger. Moreover," he continued, "I have noticed that people ceased completely to pity me at the time when Bruno left. Since then, when the two of you pass by, arm in arm, the looks that turn on me are as envious as ever they were, for now I am deemed to have sole possession of not one, but two rare and precious creatures. I know the opinion of the worldly should matter less to me than it does. I have declared my own innocence, and your chastity, to any who listen - but I know they continue to believe what it pleases them to believe."

"I have - not an ounce of feeling for you," said Newbury.

"I know it!" said Dudley. "And I could employ a crier to spend each day noising it around the court. The louder he cried, the more knowing would be the glances directed at the three of us. I stand by what I first said. I will love this son as well as I would ever have loved a child of my own flesh, so long as I have Newbury always near - to keep me honest - and to give me an air of sin."

He grinned at Newbury, and Newbury glared at him.

The more he grinned, the more she glared - and the more she glared, the more he grinned.

Cat spoke, quietly. "Do I understand you right? Do you give us your blessing?"

Dudley thought a moment. "It is not for me to bless or not. Consult with your conscience, and with God, and with each other. I have only two further things to say on the subject. First: I hope that, when our children are near, you will show only such affection with each other as Cat and I would show in their presence."

Cat nodded willingly - Newbury stiffly.

"Second, that if ever, by pure mischance, I stumble upon the two of you in full embrace: if I am slow to turn away, I ask that you will think me weak, rather than wicked."

Cat buried a smile against the still-sticky head of the infant she held, while Newbury's eyes widened, before she flushed, and spun away. She stood, hands clasped before her face, and then turned back.

"I will do as you say - I will consult with God, and with my conscience. One thing I can say now: I will love both these children as much as I can - I will teach them as well as I can."

Cat looked down at the drowsing infant in her arms, feeling finally that if she were to have, in full measure, both Dudley's love and Newbury's, she could not help but love any child dropped into her arms. And perhaps it was best, when loving a child, to have no pride of ownership - perhaps that was a snare.

She looked from one tiny face to the other, and up at all the faces that now ringed the bed, and wondered if they all could parlay their bright hopes into a fair future.

She bowed her head, finally, and implored - herself, her world, her deity, her ending, the tiny crumpled faces she regarded - "Be happy. Be happy."

Lightning Source UK Ltd.
Milton Keynes UK
UKOW04f0227110817
307090UK00001B/21/P